Physical attraction.

Pure, unadulterated lust, that was what it was.

Her body liked the idea of having sex with Joe. A lot. So much so that Maggie could feel the flush of color heating her cheeks and she had to scramble to her feet and turn her back on Joe before he carried his board and sail from the water and got close enough to see what might be a very odd expression on her face.

She had to get her head straight and make sure she never tapped into that line of thought again. If Joe knew that she had entertained any thoughts of sexual attraction to him, either he'd be horrified or he might be curious enough to make something happen. Either way, it would not only change and potentially destroy the friendship they had, it could do exactly the same thing to their working relationship.

No matter how good that sex would probably be, it wouldn't be worth it. Maggie was going to make absolutely sure that nobody knew what she'd been thinking. She wasn't even going to allow herself to think about it again.

Ever…

Dear Reader,

There's a child inside all of us, don't you think?

All it takes to remind you of that is something like a particular image or sound or smell—perhaps a whiff of the same antiseptic cream that your mom put on your knee when you fell over and grazed it—and there you are…five years old again for a tiny moment in time and feeling the comfort of being cared for. Maybe you can even feel the sting of that grazed knee!

I find it astonishing how powerful those tiny time slips can be and I know that what happens in those early years can have a profound effect on how we live our lives as adults. Maybe you use that same antiseptic cream on the knees of your own children, along with a kiss and cuddle to make "everything better."

My characters in this story have very different childhood memories, and they may be best friends, but they want very different things from life as adults. Maggie wants a big family. Joe is determined that he's not going to have a child who will have the same kind of memories he has.

One night of passion changes everything for Maggie and Joe. Stay with them as they face the new challenges in their future and I hope you find the ending as perfect as I did.

Happy reading.

With love,

Alison Roberts

PREGNANT WITH HER BEST FRIEND'S BABY

ALISON ROBERTS

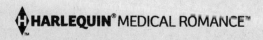

ISBN-13: 978-1-335-64159-5

Pregnant with Her Best Friend's Baby

First North American Publication 2019

Copyright © 2019 by Alison Roberts

Printed in U.S.A.

Visit the Author Profile page
at Harlequin.com for more titles.

**Praise for
Alison Roberts**

"The emotional connection I had to this story was
strong and unique. It squeezed my heart, captured
my mind, and will stay with me for a while."

—*Goodreads* on *Their First Family Christmas*

CHAPTER ONE

'DO YOU KNOW what the French word for a midwife is, Joe?' Maggie Lewis jammed her helmet over her blonde curls but let the ends of her chinstrap dangle as they strode swiftly out to the helipad.

'What's that got to do with anything?' Maggie's crew partner, Joe Wallace, pulled open the side door of the helicopter, briefly obscuring the logo of Wellington's Aratika Rescue Service emblazoned on the side of the aircraft.

'We're going to a woman in labour.'

'Ah…is that what it is? Hasn't come through on my pager yet.'

'Prolonged first stage,' Maggie added. 'And the midwife has called for assistance because she's now caught up with another patient who's having a miscarriage and she can't get back to check on this woman any-time soon.'

Joe stood back to let Maggie climb on board first. Their pilot, Andy, was already in the cockpit, well into an automatic preflight routine with the crewman and co-pilot Nick sitting beside him. The rotors were gathering speed and the downdraught was enough to make Joe push his sun-streaked brown hair back off his forehead and out of his eyes before he pulled his helmet on. How was it that he always managed to look as if he was overdue for a haircut?

Maggie fastened her chinstrap as she sat down and then pulled her harness over her shoulders. 'Anyway… I'm sure you don't know what a midwife is in French, so I'll tell you. It's a *sage-femme*. Direct translation is actually "wise woman".'

'Ah…' Joe was grinning as he pulled the door shut behind him. 'I see where this is going. You want to take the lead on this one, don't you, even though it's my turn? And even though you had all the fun of the post-cardiac arrest case we just finished?'

'It was a good case, wasn't it?' Maggie smiled back as she pulled down her microphone, responding affirmatively to Andy's query about whether they were good to go and then watching the ground recede as they lifted into the air. She was still thinking about their last mission, however. 'It's not often you get to bring someone back to life enough to have them cracking jokes with the ED staff when we get there.'

'But you want this one, too.'

'I was a midwife, once upon a time, you know. One of those wise women.'

'Last century, you mean?'

'Hey...you're older than me, mate. I wouldn't go making ageist jokes if I were you.'

'At least I knew I wanted to be a paramedic from the get-go. You had to be a nurse and then a midwife before you saw the light and found your true calling.'

'I must have been crazy,' Maggie muttered. 'I could be working in a nice, fully equipped maternity unit with colleagues who appreciate me and...*whoa*...watch out for those potholes, Andy.'

'Sorry.' But their pilot chuckled. 'It might be a bit of a bumpy ride today. That's Windy Wellington for you.'

'I *do* appreciate you, Maggie,' Joe said a few seconds later. He sounded perfectly sincere but Maggie could still hear a grin in his voice. 'You know that, don't you?'

She shrugged. Joe had been one of the first people she had worked with on the base when she'd joined the crew five years ago. 'You've put up with me long enough, I guess.'

'And there I was thinking it was you who was putting up with me.'

For a second, they caught each other's gaze, with the ease and familiarity that only came after a friendship had had years to gather strength along with the kind of depth that could only come from shared experiences that often involved a life or death struggle. Their banter might push the limits occasionally but the trust and respect between Maggie and Joe was rock solid.

'Actually…' Andy's voice coming through the in-built headphones in their helmets broke that moment of connection. 'It's me who's had to put up with both of you for years now. Years and years of listening to you bicker about who gets to lead which job.'

'We're the dream team,' Joe informed him. 'As well you know.'

'Yeah, yeah… I'm going to toss a coin when we land. Whoever gets heads gets to lead, okay?'

Maggie and Joe shared another swift

glance. They both knew it wouldn't actually make any difference. Neither of them had the kind of ego that interfered with clear communication or with deferring to someone who was more skilled in a particular area. They really were a 'dream team' and, while there were many medics on the Aratika Rescue Base that Maggie loved to work with, Joe was definitely her favourite.

'It's not as though we're likely to have to deal with a delivery, anyway,' Joe added. 'If the mother's had a prolonged first stage she'll be exhausted and may not be anywhere near fully dilated. She might end up having a Caesarean. It's the midwife's call to get her into hospital instead of continuing with a home birth. I guess she's requested a chopper because it's an isolated property.'

'Long, unsealed road to the nearest highway, too,' the crewman, Nick, put in. 'I don't imagine a bumpy road like that would be very good for a woman in labour.'

Another pocket of turbulence made Maggie reach for a handhold. 'At this rate, the ride with us into hospital might speed things up as much as a road trip could.'

'We should be out of the worst of it when we get up north a bit,' Andy told them. 'ETA's twenty minutes.'

Maggie peered down at the rugged, forest-covered hills and nearby coastline beneath them.

'Isn't that the Castle Cliffs resort down there?'

'Where Cooper and Fizz are having their wedding?' Joe leaned sideways to see where Maggie was pointing to a group of buildings half-hidden by forest on the edge of a cliff top. Cooper had started working at the base six months ago after emigrating from Scotland and Fizz was one of the emergency medicine specialists who were part of Aratika's elite staff.

'I think it must be.' Joe nodded. 'Certainly looks like the only way to get to it is by four-wheel drive or chopper.'

'I might take my bike.'

'What—you're not going to wear a dress?' Joe sounded shocked.

Maggie sighed. 'I suppose I'd better. I hadn't thought about it yet.'

'The wedding's next weekend. You'd better get on with it.'

'I know. It's just happened in a bit of a rush, you know? I really wasn't expecting Fizz to suddenly get so formal. She told me not so long ago that she was never going to get married again.'

'I guess finding out they're going to have a baby changed things. Not that that's the best reason to decide to tie the knot.' There was an odd note in Joe's voice.

'It's as good a reason as any,' Maggie responded. 'And I've never seen either of them looking so happy.'

Joe's grunt was reluctant agreement. 'Yeah... I would have thought Fizz would have been more upset having to give up her shifts at Aratika but I've not seen the smile drop from her face once.'

'Mmm...' Maggie closed her eyes for a moment. She could imagine how happy Fizz was feeling. Not just because she'd won that life lottery of finding the person she wanted to be with for ever—something Maggie had failed to find yet—but with the anticipation of holding their first baby in her arms in the near future. Maggie's own arms were loosely folded in front of her and she could actually feel an emptiness there. An ache of longing...

It was getting stronger, that longing. The ticking of a biological clock. One of Mother Nature's tricks to persuade women to reproduce before it became too late and, at nearly thirty-six, Maggie knew that her window of opportunity to become a mother easily was starting to close. She'd been envious of Fizz when she'd heard the news. Dead jealous, if she was really honest with herself.

'That's the road we're looking for down there.' Andy's voice broke into Maggie's thoughts a few minutes later. 'We'll follow it but keep an eye out for a farmhouse with a red ute parked in front of it. Apparently there's an empty paddock by the road that we can land in.'

'I'm getting an update.' Joe was reading his pager. 'Our patient is a thirty-one-year-old first-time mum. No problems with pregnancy and she's full term. Name's Kathy Price.'

It wasn't Kathy who met them at the door of the house a few minutes later but her husband, Darren, who looked like he'd just come in from working on the farm. He had a checked shirt on over a pair of shorts and he dropped a pair of boots onto the veranda of the farmhouse before inviting the paramedic crew to come inside.

'Dunno what all this fuss is about,' he said, as he led them through to a bedroom. 'I could have driven Kath in to the hospital. We don't need all these bells and whistles.'

'I think Kathy's midwife was a bit concerned about how tired your wife was sounding,' Joe said calmly. 'And it is quite a drive.'

Maggie was slipping her arms out of her backpack straps. She crouched down beside the bed.

'Hi, Kathy. My name's Maggie and that's Joe. We've come to take you into hospital to have your baby on your midwife's advice. Are you happy with that decision?'

The exhausted-looking young woman nodded. 'I'm just so tired,' she whispered. 'It's been going on since the middle of last night.'

'Your midwife checked you this morning, yes?'

'Yeah…and I was two centimetres dilated at ten o'clock. She came back after lunch at one o'clock and I'd only got to four centimetres by then.'

'So…' Maggie checked her watch. 'That's about four hours ago now. How often are you having contractions?'

Kathy rolled her head from side to side. 'I'm not sure. It feels like every couple of minutes and…and it hurts. I know I said I didn't want any pain relief in my birth plan but I didn't know it was going to hurt this much.'

'We can give you something for the pain.'

Maggie glanced at where Joe was opening their packs and readying the equipment that they might need. A birthing pack that included neonatal resuscitation items like the miniature airways and bag mask. IV gear. Their small tanks of oxygen and Entonox. 'We'll start with some Entonox but we'll put a line in your hand, if you're happy with that, so we can give you something stronger if you need it.'

'He's a big baby.' Darren sounded proud. 'They said that at the last scan.'

'Oh?' An alarm bell sounded a warning for Maggie. 'How big?'

'Not too big,' Kathy said. 'My midwife said it was below the limit for it being a problem for a home birth and we both wanted that.'

'Birth's a natural process.' Darren nodded. 'Why go near a hospital if you don't have to?'

'You can't just tie a rope around a hoof and pull it out,' Kathy snapped at her husband. 'I'm not one of your sheep. Ow…it's starting again.' She dropped her head back against the pillows and groaned. 'It *hurts*… and…and I feel *sick*…'

Joe was right beside Maggie now. He

raised an eyebrow. 'Transition?' he suggested quietly.

Kathy was shaking as the contraction subsided. 'I need to go to the toilet,' she moaned.

'It's okay, Kathy,' Maggie said reassuringly. 'I think that perhaps you're a bit closer to having your baby than we thought. I'm going to get your clothes off and see what's happening, okay? Joe's going to take your blood pressure and things and...' She caught Joe's gaze. 'Let's get some oxygen on, shall we? And it would be great to get a foetal heart rate.'

'What's going on?' Darren asked as they worked over Kathy. 'I thought you were just going to take us in to the hospital.'

'That was the initial plan,' Maggie replied as she cut clothing clear. 'But we can't transport Kathy if a birth is imminent. We can manage things a lot better here than in the back of a helicopter.'

'Crikey...' Darren's face became noticeably paler. 'It's happening now?' He moved to the head of the bed to lean over his wife. 'You okay, hon?'

'No...' Kathy grabbed at his hand. 'Where's that gas? I can't do this... I need to *push*...'

'Wow...you're crowning, Kathy.' Maggie

could see the dark whorls of damp hair on the baby's head. 'Your baby's almost here… Keep pushing—you're doing great.'

Joe had the blood-pressure cuff wrapped around Kathy's arm and the bulb in his hand but gave up trying to take a reading as he leaned to see what Maggie was watching.

They both saw the moment that it happened. The baby's head was almost born and then it pulled back like a turtle retreating into its shell.

'Turtle sign,' Maggie said very quietly. She glanced up to catch Joe's gaze. They both knew that this had the potential to become an obstetric emergency in a very short space of time.

'Don't push any more for the moment, Kathy,' Maggie said calmly. 'Try and pant for the rest of this contraction. Darren? Can you take Kathy's pillows away? We need to get her lying as flat as possible.'

Maggie was going to hold the baby's head and apply some gentle traction with the next contraction. Kathy was red-faced and gasping as she pushed. This time the baby's head came a little further but then it stopped.

'What's going on?' Darren looked fearful as he looked up from the baby to meet Maggie's gaze. 'Why isn't it coming out?'

It was an effort to keep her voice this calm, especially as Kathy started sobbing. 'Baby's shoulders are just a bit caught behind the bones at the bottom of Kathy's pelvis.'

Darren put his arms around his wife. 'It'll be okay, hon. These guys know what they're doing.'

'*Why* is this happening?' Kathy cried. 'After all this time and it's been so hard… it's not *fair*…'

'It could be a positional thing,' Maggie said. 'Or maybe your baby's a bit bigger than the scan suggested. Don't worry, we have several ways we can help.'

And less than five minutes in which to do so.

Joe was right beside her and they were able to talk quietly for a few moments as Darren tried to comfort and reassure Kathy as she sobbed.

'We can only spend about thirty seconds on each manoeuvre to deal with shoulder dystocia,' Maggie said. 'I know the protocol but I'd like to get some expert obstetric backup on the radio.' She lowered her voice even further. 'We need to be prepared for a neonatal resuscitation, too.'

Joe reached for the radio clipped to his belt but he was still listening to Maggie. 'We'll try the McRoberts manoeuvre first. If that doesn't work, I'll need you to provide traction while I put on some suprapubic pressure.'

Maggie turned to Darren. 'Help me move Kathy down towards the end of the bed,' she told him. 'And, Kathy? I want you to pull your knees up to your chest and then push as hard as you can with your next contraction.'

Even as she was encouraging Kathy to push and telling her how well she was doing, Maggie's brain was racing through the next steps, which would mean applying pressure to try and move the baby's shoulders both externally and then internally. If that didn't work she would have to follow guidance from one of the consultants in the maternity wing of Wellington's Royal Hospital. She didn't want to have to think about the more drastic measures that might need to be taken or the risks to both baby and mother.

Joe caught Maggie's gaze as the sounds of the effort Kathy was putting into pushing began to fade into exhausted groans. Maggie nodded and they shifted positions, with Joe gently taking hold of the baby's head and Maggie moving to the side of the bed where she could feel for the position of the baby's shoulders.

'You're going to feel me pushing this time as well,' she told Kathy. 'We need the biggest push you've got this time.'

'I can't,' Kathy moaned. 'I can't do it…'

'Yes, you can.' Darren was lying across the top of the bed, holding both of Kathy's hands. 'Hang on tight…you've got this…'

Maggie could feel the curve of the baby's back beneath her fingers and then the lump of the tiny shoulder. She locked her hands by weaving her fingers together and then put the heel of one hand just above the shoulder. As Kathy's next contraction gathered strength and she started to push, Maggie pressed down on the baby's shoulder. Joe was applying traction. At one point during the tense thirty seconds of effort, Maggie and Joe held eye contact with each other. They coordinated a rocking motion as Kathy's contraction began to recede and, finally, Maggie could feel the movement beneath her hands as one shoulder and then the other was freed.

'Keep it going,' she urged Kathy. 'Just a little bit more… Baby's coming… *Push*, Kathy *push*…you can do it…'

And there was the baby, in Joe's hands. Looking…alarmingly limp. Maggie reached for the clamps and sterile scissors from the birthing pack roll. They needed to cut the cord fast if resuscitation was needed.

'Is he okay?' Kathy was trying to push herself up onto her elbows. 'What's happening…?'

'He's breathing,' Joe told her. 'And starting to move. I'm just going to check his heart rate.'

The baby was moving and screwing up his little face as though he wanted to cry but couldn't find the energy yet. They were both good signs but his colour wasn't great, with his extremities a dark shade of blue, and Maggie wasn't sure that his breathing was adequate. Joe wasn't looking too worried, however. He was smiling down at the baby as he dried it off with a soft towel.

'Hey there, little guy. You going to tell us what you think about all this?'

Maggie had the cord clamped and the scissors in her hand but, if an urgent resuscitation wasn't needed, she didn't have to rush.

'Darren? Do you want to cut the cord?'

'Apgar six at one minute,' Joe told her. 'Heart rate is over a hundred but the resp rate is on the slow side and he's pretty blue.'

By the time Darren had cut through the cord, the baby was starting to make sounds. The first warbling cry came a few seconds later and Kathy burst into tears and held out her arms.

'Can I hold him? Please?'

Again, Maggie and Joe shared a glance. And a smile this time. This situation was under control now with the emergency delivery successfully managed. Kathy still needed careful monitoring because she was at more risk of a postpartum haemorrhage after the complication with her baby's delivery, and she needed to transfer to an obstetric unit as quickly as possible. But keeping the baby warm was also a priority and the best way to do that was to have him skin to skin with his mother and to cover them both with warm blankets.

It was Maggie who scooped up the infant to place him in Kathy's arms and, as she felt the weight of the newborn in her own arms and against her own breast, she felt oddly close to tears. Because it was a reminder of that ache of emptiness she'd been so aware of earlier when she'd been thinking of the baby her friend Fizz was going to have?

No. These were more like tears of joy. How precious was this new life? Especially this one, after giving them all a fright on his way into the world, but all babies were just amazing and the joy of being part of a delivery was something that would never grow old.

This was more than a purely professional satisfaction, however. Maybe there was an echo of that ache of longing. Of the emptiness. Not in her arms that were still full of this new life but somewhere further down in Maggie's body—in the space where a baby of her own might grow one day.

Her smile was definitely a bit wobbly as she helped Kathy move her clothing and gather her baby onto her chest.

'He's just gorgeous,' Maggie murmured, stepping back to let Darren get close to his wife and baby for a few precious minutes of family bonding time as she and Joe got packed up and ready for the transfer to hospital.

Darren sounded a lot closer to tears than Maggie was. 'Looks just like his daddy, I reckon,' he said. 'How 'bout that?'

Maggie checked her watch as she rapidly assessed the baby again before turning away to give this brand-new family just a moment of relative privacy. 'Apgar score eight at five minutes,' she told Joe.

He nodded, grinning, and then stripped off his gloves and unclipped his radio. 'Andy? We'll be ready to go inside ten minutes.

Crank up the central heating in the cabin, we've got a baby to keep warm on the way home.'

Darren overheard him. 'Will there be room for a dad in the helicopter as well?'

'Sorry, mate.' Joe shook his head. 'It's going to be a bit crowded. You'll need to follow us by road.'

'Don't worry,' Maggie added, to soften the blow. 'We're going to take very good care of both Kathy and the baby.'

A medical team, including Fizz Wilson, was waiting on one side of the Royal's rooftop helipad to take over Kathy's care as soon as they landed and lifted out the stretcher.

'Third stage happened en route,' Maggie told Fizz. 'Oxytocin was administered on scene after the birth but I would estimate blood loss with the delivery of the placenta was still around three hundred mils with ongoing but slower loss now. She's on her second litre of normal saline. Blood pressure's one hundred and five over fifty.'

'I feel fine,' Kathy said. 'Just a bit tired, that's all.'

But Fizz took note of the low blood pressure and the urgent need to control any ongoing bleeding.

'Let's get moving,' she instructed the ED staff with her. 'Maggie, can you bring the baby, please? We've got a paediatric team waiting for him downstairs.'

Maggie followed Kathy's stretcher with Joe walking beside her. 'I could get used to this,' she said.

'What? Having full-on cases with successful outcomes? That's two today.' Joe was smiling. 'I could get used to it, too.'

'No… I mean *this*…' Maggie looked down at the tiny sleeping face visible amongst the folds of blanket in her arms. 'Carrying a baby around. I think I want one.'

Joe made a shuddering sound. 'Rather you than me, mate. Hey…' He increased his pace as the stretcher was slotted into the rooftop elevator. 'Is there room for us in there, too?'

They squeezed in.

Fizz was right beside Maggie. She had her gaze fixed on monitor screen of the life pack, taking in as much information about Kathy's condition as she could, but she slid a quick sideways glance at the baby a moment later.

'Any problems?'

'Not at all. He was a bit flat to start with but he picked up quickly. Apgar score was ten at ten minutes.'

Fizz was smiling as she turned back to her

patient. 'He's so cute,' she told Kathy. 'Have you decided on a name yet?'

'I like Aiden,' Kathy said. 'But Darren wants him to be Patrick, after his dad. We decided we'd wait and see what suited him more.' She twisted her head, trying to see her baby's face. 'I think he looks like an Aiden, don't you?'

Maggie smiled. 'Aiden's a great name.' But so was Patrick, she thought. One of her favourite boy's names, in fact. She wondered if Fizz and Cooper had already started discussing possible names for their baby or if they knew whether it was a girl or a boy.

The elevator doors opened again as they reached the ground floor and Fizz stayed by the head of the stretcher as it was swiftly rolled towards a resuscitation area in the emergency department. Kathy would have no idea that her doctor was pregnant, Maggie thought. And here she was, with baby Aiden or Patrick still in her arms. It was baby overload today, that was for sure.

Her head was still full of it when she and Joe finally got to take a break and sat down in the staffroom of the Aratika Rescue Base.

'I haven't finished the paperwork for the post-cardiac arrest case yet, let alone for the birth,' Maggie sighed.

'It won't take too long,' Joe said. 'I'll do the cardiac one.'

'Because it's half-done already?'

'No. Because you're the one who wants a baby. This way, you get to enjoy the case all over again.'

'Hmm…' Maggie shook her head. 'It could have turned out to be not very enjoyable at all. I was so relieved the moment I felt that shoulder start to move.'

'I'll bet.' Joe pulled the folder of paperwork towards him and took a pen from the pocket of his overalls. 'Keep it in mind when you choose the father of your baby. You're so short, it might be wise not to marry a solid, over six foot tall farmer like Kathy did.'

'Five foot four is not short. I'm average,' Maggie countered. 'And I don't even know any farmers. Or any potential baby daddies at all, in fact.'

'They're out there. In droves. You just haven't been looking.'

'That's because I got fed up with relationships that were going nowhere fast.'

Including the one she'd been in with Richard, years ago, when Maggie had first started working at the rescue base. One that had had a promising start but had ebbed into being nothing more than flatmates. Friends. And it hadn't been enough for either of them.

'Maybe that's because you go into them expecting them to *be* going somewhere. That can scare guys off, you know. It would scare the hell out of me, that's for sure. In fact, it's precisely why I'm currently single again.'

Maggie snorted. 'It's a baby I want. A partner would be a bonus, of course, but I'm running out of time to jump through all those hoops.' She was only half joking. It really did feel like she was running out of time, given how many dead ends she had already come up against in the search to find someone to share her life with. 'And who says you have to *marry* someone to have a baby, anyway? You might marry someone and end up being a single mother anyway— like Laura.' Her flatmate had escaped what she suspected might have been an abusive relationship years ago when her son, Harrison, was only a tiny baby.

'So you're going to do the independent professional woman thing and go to a sperm bank or something?'

Maggie blinked. 'D'you know, I hadn't actually thought of that.'

'Why not? You read about people doing it all the time. Especially older, professional women who choose not to get married or realise they're running out of time. People just like you. And it seems like a great way to get a designer baby. You could practically choose its hair colour and how smart it'll be.' But Joe was frowning now. 'Of course, you're going to provide the other half of the genes so it might just come out with blonde hair and blue eyes and to be not very…' His lips twitched.

Maggie threw her pen at him. 'Are you trying to tell me that I'm not very smart?'

Joe had already caught the pen. 'I was only going to say you're not very tall.'

Maggie narrowed her eyes. 'Not sure I believe that. And what did you mean by "something"?'

'Huh?'

'You said a sperm bank "or something".'

'Oh…' Joe picked up his coffee cup and took a swallow. 'You could just pick someone you liked the look of, I guess, lay on the charm and lure them home and hope that he's not too careful about birth control.'

'*Joe*… How irresponsible would that be?'

'Irresponsible on the part of the guy, that's true.' Joe shook his head. 'I'd never relinquish that responsibility.'

'I couldn't get pregnant and not tell someone that they were going to be a father. That's just not right.'

'I guess.' Joe was focussing on the paperwork in front of him now. 'Do what I read about a gay couple doing recently, then. The women asked one of their good friends and he agreed to be the donor. He said he wanted them to have their family and he was happy to be a kind of uncle but never wanted to be a father.'

They both concentrated on the paperwork for a while but, even as Maggie filled in the precise details relating to the obstetric case that was clearly going to be the last job for their shift today, another line of thought was ticking along somewhere in the background of her brain.

Thoughts about sperm banks. How easy was it to get accepted for treatment and how expensive it might be. And how it worked. Did you have a wish list of things to tick off, like physical characteristics of height and hair colour or evidence of intelligence such as a university qualification? What about more important attributes like whether someone could make you laugh or how kind he was?

Thoughts about the other things Joe had suggested circled in her mind, too. Randomly picking some guy with the intention of seducing him and possibly lying about being on birth control was not an acceptable option but…but the idea of using a co-operative friend, now that *was* interesting…

So interesting that it was the only thing Maggie was thinking about as she kicked her bike into life and threaded her way through the city traffic not long after her conversation with Joe.

By the time she was getting into bed that night, it had started to feel like it was her own idea.

And, out of all the men she knew, there was only one that stood out as a perfect possibility.

Joe Wallace.

The thought of broaching the subject was a bit nerve-racking. Enough so to keep Maggie awake for quite some time. On the positive side, he'd had a half-smile on his face when he'd said 'rather you than me' when she'd been holding Kathy's baby, and had said she wanted one as well, so maybe he was on the same page as that co-operative friend he'd told her about—who didn't want to become a father but was happy to be a kind of uncle.

On the other side of that coin, however,

was the fact that she'd be stepping into a realm that had never been there with Joe and that was why their friendship was so solid. They'd both been in long-term relationships when they'd first met as colleagues. By the time they were single, they were already good friends and Maggie had learned the hard way that friendship was not enough to base a long-term relationship on. Joe was off limits and he clearly felt exactly the same way and that had never been a problem. But baby-making, no matter how you ended up actually doing it, had everything to do with sex and even the thought of opening that conversation with Joe was enough to make Maggie blush.

But it wasn't enough to make her dismiss what seemed to be a perfect plan. As she drifted off to sleep Maggie's thoughts were tumbling, interwoven with memories that went back so far they were no more than misty glimpses. She'd had an old-fashioned child-sized pram when she was very little and she would cram every doll and teddy bear she owned into that pram and wheel it everywhere.

My babies, she would tell everyone.

When she was older she had her fashion dolls that gave her a mother and father figure and she would add smaller dolls as their children. Lots and lots of children because that was what made a 'real' family. It wasn't that she hadn't been happy and loved as an only child, it was just that she knew it was a case of the more the merrier. Her parents had desperately wanted more children and had been sad that it hadn't happened but it hadn't dented the rock-solid love they shared. They would be the best grandparents ever.

That was something else that Maggie wanted, of course. A relationship that was as perfect a match as her parents' one was. The 'love at first sight' whirlwind romance like the one they'd told her about so many times and starting a life together that would get better and better as they got older. It wasn't that Maggie hadn't found the 'love at first sight' type of thing, it was just that any whirlwind romance eventually crashed and burned and she'd been let down so many times that, for the moment at least, she was giving up.

That desire for a family of her own had never vanished, though. In the last moments before sleep claimed Maggie, she could feel the intensity of that longing that morphed from a pram full of beloved toys to the feeling of holding a real, live baby in her arms, as she'd done today.

There was something a bit weird happening.

Joe couldn't put his finger on it but, as the day wore on, he wondered if it was because Maggie seemed even bouncier than normal. More enthusiastic. More…smiley…

Several times, he caught her opening her mouth as if she was about to say something and then snapping it shut and throwing herself into whatever task she was doing on their downtime, like reading a journal article or washing up some dishes. It wasn't until they were in the locker room, when their shift had finished, that Joe finally gave up. The way Maggie was looking at him felt like the heat of a laser in the middle of his back as he pulled what he needed from his locker.

He turned his head. 'You've been staring at me all day. What's going on?'

'Sorry…' Maggie smiled brightly at him. 'There's something I wanted to ask you, that's all. I was…um…waiting for the best moment.'

'Now's good.' Joe smiled back. If Maggie

wanted a favour, then he was her man. Always. 'Shoot.'

'Um…' She was fishing in her locker, putting things into a shoulder bag. Her voice sounded as if she was trying hard to keep it casual. 'It's about what you said. Yesterday. When I was talking about wanting a baby?'

'What did I say?' Joe tried to think back. 'Oh…you mean about sperm banks?'

'No…' Maggie's hands stilled. 'About asking a friend.'

'Oh…' He liked that she'd liked his idea. It was always great to find a solution to a mate's problem. 'Glad I could help.' He unhooked his jacket from the back of his locker. 'So who's the lucky guy, then?' He raised an eyebrow in Maggie's direction when she didn't answer. 'Your potential baby daddy? Is it Jack?'

'Jack's my flatmate. How awkward would that be?'

'Don?'

'Shh…' Maggie threw a glance over her shoulder, checking that they were still alone in the locker room. Her cheeks had reddened even at the idea of their boss being involved.

'Who, then?'

He could see the way Maggie swallowed hard, as if what she was about to say was terribly important. He could see how wide her eyes were as well. Shining with something that looked very like hope. The hairs on the back of his neck prickled as they rose.

'You, Joe,' she whispered. 'You're the person I'd choose out of everybody I've ever known.'

He should have seen it coming, perhaps, but he hadn't and it hit him like a steam train. The blast of remembering what it was like to be a child that hadn't been wanted. The absolute determination to never, ever be on the other side of that coin—the father who hadn't wanted that child.

Joe could feel the colour draining out of his face. He could see the reflection of his own horror in Maggie's eyes. She knew she'd made a terrible mistake but she had no idea how to go about fixing it. He could solve this problem. Just make a joke and brush it off.

Except he couldn't. The words had been said and couldn't be unsaid and they had touched such a very deep chord within him. The idea of him casually—*deliberately*—fathering a child was hanging in the air between them. Totally abhorrent. Totally unacceptable. Joe couldn't begin to find any words to let Maggie know just how shocked he was but maybe he didn't need to. She was looking rather pale herself.

Embarrassed. Mortified, even.

For once, Joe had no inclination to make her feel any better. He shook his head, slammed his locker door shut and was walking out as if it was simply an ordinary end to their run of days working together.

'See ya,' he muttered, without meeting her gaze. 'Enjoy your days off.'

CHAPTER TWO

'WOW…CHECK YOU OUT, Maggie. You're wearing a *dress*…'

'Hi, Jack… Yeah, I know… I'm just trying to decide if I want to keep it.'

Maggie had spent half her afternoon off
today shopping for something suitable to
wear to a wedding but it felt very odd having all this loose fabric brushing against her
lower legs. Just how long had it been since
she'd tapped into her feminine side and worn
a dress instead of her uniform or jeans or the
leather pants she wore for protection when
she rode her beloved Harley-Davidson sport-
ster motorbike with its sky-blue fuel tank
and mudguards?

She turned back to where their other flatmate, Laura, was sitting on the couch, Harrison snuggled up beside her. They were both
staring at her thoughtfully so she did a bit
of a twirl, one way and then the other. That

was enough to make her wonder how long it had been since she'd been anywhere near a dance floor. At least a year, she decided. About when her last relationship had faded into oblivion after a few months had made it obvious it should never have got going in the first place. That 'love at first sight' wasn't to be trusted. Maggie stifled a sigh.

'So…what do you think?'

'It's perfect,' Laura pronounced. 'That blue is exactly the same colour as your eyes and I love the little daisy print. Very summery.' She ruffled her son's hair. 'What do you think, Harry? Doesn't Maggie look pretty? Isn't it fun that we're all going to get dressed up for the wedding tomorrow?'

Harry wrinkled his nose. 'I don't want to get dressed up.'

'You don't have to get *really* dressed up. It's not a fancy wedding where you might have to wear a suit, but you have got an important job to do. You get to carry the rings.'

'I'd get dressed up,' Jack told him, 'if I could go. I'd wear my very best jeans and a shirt.'

'A T-shirt?'

'No, a real shirt. With buttons. Maybe even a tie.'

'Why can't you go?'

'I wish I could but I have to work, buddy. Someone has to be ready to go up in a helicopter or off on a bike and look after the people who get sick or injured.'

And Jack probably hadn't even tried to juggle his roster to take time off. He'd only recently succeeded in winning one of the hotly contested paramedic jobs on the rescue base and his excitement was still palpable.

'Who were you crewed with today?' Laura asked. 'I didn't see anyone from Aratika come into Emergency during my shift.'

'It was a really quiet day. Joe and I got a bit bored, to be honest. And we ate far too many of Shirley's cookies. I'm meeting him at the gym as soon as I've collected my gear to try and burn some that sugar load off.'

'How come Joe was working?' Maggie asked. 'He's on the same roster as me.'

'He was covering for Adam, who called in sick. Food poisoning or some kind of gastro bug. I hope he's back on deck tomorrow. Joe said he could come in again but he wouldn't want to miss the wedding.'

'No...' But Maggie could hear the doubtful note in her own voice.

Maybe Joe had a reason that meant he wouldn't be too upset to miss the wedding.

Or rather, to miss having to spend any time with Maggie.

She hadn't seen him since the last shift they had worked together. Since that awful moment when she'd made the cringeworthy mistake of telling him that she wanted him to father a baby for her.

'I reckon if Cooper had decided to have a best man, it would have been Joe,' Jack added.

'Yes,' Laura agreed. 'And then Maggie would have been a bridesmaid for Fizz.'

Thank goodness their friends weren't going down such a traditional format for their wedding. How awkward could that have been, with everyone they worked with watching them? Someone would have picked up on the odd vibe between the best man and the bridesmaid and maybe asked what the problem was, which would have only ramped up this odd tension.

There hadn't been any chance to try and convince Joe that the notion of him being a sperm donor had only been a joke because the night shift crew had been outside chatting to their pilot as Maggie had followed behind Joe, who had got into his car and simply driven past, with a casual wave. Maggie had texted him later with what seemed a slightly awkward attempt to tell him he had nothing to worry about but the response had been a terse 'Forget about it, I already have', which didn't quite ring true.

It was probably unfortunate that their days off had meant they hadn't had to work together the following day. It would have been so much easier to brush off and genuinely forget about it if they hadn't both had a couple of days to think about it.

Because Maggie was quite sure that Joe *would* have been thinking about it, even if it wasn't filling his mind to quite the same extent as it was hers. Who wouldn't have to give it some thought, when confronted by something you would never have expected your friend to come out with? Something that had clearly shocked him. She couldn't text him again, either, because that would be making it into a bigger thing than it actually was. All they needed was to be in the same space, an opportunity to make a joke about it and then they could go back to the way things had always been—a friendship that made it possible to work and socialise together and to always feel perfectly safe.

'Anyway...' Maggie pasted a bright smile on her face. 'Even though I'm not a bridesmaid, I think I will wear a dress. *This* dress.'

'Good choice.' Laura encouraged Harrison to slide off the couch but kept hold of his hand as she got up. 'Want to help Mummy decide what she's going to wear?'

'I'm tired...' Harrison was climbing back onto the couch. 'Can I watch TV?'

'I'll help Mummy choose,' Maggie offered. 'Let's both go girly with pretty dresses. How often do we get the chance to do that?'

'Almost never,' Laura said. She was smiling now, too. 'It's going to be a great day,' she added. 'I can't wait.'

Maggie had to stop herself crossing her fingers, the way she used to when she was a kid and believed that the gesture excused you if you were about to tell an outright lie.

'Me, too.'

'You're a brave man, Cooper Sinclair.'

'Why is that, Joe?' His colleague was grinning. 'Because I'm taking the plunge and getting married?'

'Nah... You're on a hilltop in famously windy Wellington and you're wearing a skirt.'

It was more than a hilltop. They were actually standing on the top of a cliff, with a spectacular view of the sea and islands through the archway that would frame the ceremony due to begin shortly. And, yes, while it was a gloriously sunny day, the currents of air were enough to be stirring the hemline of the kilt Cooper was wearing.

Cooper snorted. 'What else would a Scotsman wear for the happiest day of his life?' He wasn't looking at Joe, however. His gaze was fixed on the Castle Cliff resort buildings and he obviously couldn't wait to catch the first glimpse of his bride coming to meet him. He glanced at his watch then—a nervous gesture that was completely out of character.

'It's time…'

'I'd better find a seat, then.' Joe left his friend standing alone and headed for the far side of the last row of white seats that had been arranged in a semi-circle facing the archway. He wasn't at all bothered that the first rows were already full of settled guests. He was happy to be attending this celebration but he didn't want to be too close to the action. Weddings made him a little nervous, too. Didn't Cooper and Fizz realise what a huge risk they were taking? How high the chances were that it wasn't going to turn out to be happy-ever-after? And they had decided to get married because there was a baby on the way. Not that he was going to say anything but it felt a bit close to a death knell to Joe.

Just before he turned to sit down, he noticed another kilt-clad figure appear on an upper balcony of the resort building, a set of bagpipes cradled in his arms. At the same time, three figures were hurrying down the steps from the lower veranda, two of them wearing dresses. The other was a small boy and Joe knew that it must be Laura's son, Harrison, who was apparently in charge of the wedding rings. Laura had to be watching over her son, as she always did, and that meant that the other woman was most likely her flatmate and close friend. He didn't really need the glimpse of sunlight catching blonde curls to light them up like a halo to confirm his guess.

Maggie…

Joe sat down with a thump and fixed his gaze on the scene ahead of him, where the celebrant had joined Cooper.

The level of discomfort Joe was aware of now was far greater than anything weddings normally engendered. He hadn't seen Maggie for days. Hadn't *wanted* to see her after that shocking conversation at the end of their last shift together, and as the time apart was increasing, so was the level of…

what…awkwardness? Certainly tension, anyway.

It wasn't something he'd ever been aware of with Maggie. She was, in fact, probably the only woman he ever felt completely at ease with. Other than Shirley, of course, but the self-appointed housekeeper of the Aratika Rescue Base was a mother figure for everyone there, with zero risk of her wanting anything inappropriate from her relationship with Joe. He'd thought his friendship with Maggie was just as sacrosanct. That they were real friends who trusted each other and that there was no threat of the usual sexual tension that inevitably seemed to develop when he tried to be simply friends with a woman.

The other seats in this back row were filling up quickly from the aisle side as people realised the ceremony was about to start. Joe noticed Don, the base manager, take a seat and then Tom, one of the emergency department consultants at the Royal, took the next seat, leaving only two spaces. Tom was becoming more involved with the base, having taken over the shifts Fizz had had to relinquish when she'd discovered she was pregnant. Laura went past Joe on the other side, holding Harrison's hand, leading him to where a seat had been saved in the front row, and then there was a swish of blue fabric right in front of Joe.

'Excuse me.'

He pulled his feet closer as Maggie edged past his knees. Seeing Laura and Harrison had been a reminder of the example of successful single parenthood that Maggie was inspired by and that was yet another sharp reminder of the awkwardness that now lay between them. The fact that she was choosing to sit beside him came as something of a relief. Perhaps they could get past what was threatening to be an elephant in the room when they next had the opportunity to talk to each other, let alone the next time they had to work together.

Except that a quick glance showed that the empty seats beside Joe were the only ones available and Maggie chose the one next to Tom, leaving an empty seat between herself and Joe. She flicked him a quick smile of greeting but then turned to say hello to Tom and the slightly nervous way she had avoided more than a split second of eye contact gave Joe an odd jolt of something that he couldn't define but which he definitely didn't like.

Wow...how could a simple, white chair

that wasn't even solid suddenly feel like an impenetrable barrier?

The mournful wail of the bagpipe music starting in the background only added to the sensation that something had changed. Or been lost? Something potentially huge?

Like everyone else, Joe turned his head to watch Fizz come out onto the veranda and then walk down the steps towards the central aisle that led to the archway where Cooper was waiting. It was no surprise that she wasn't wearing a white dress. Joe knew that she'd been there and done that once already and that her first husband had been tragically killed in an accident on their honeymoon. Maybe it wasn't even surprising that she'd chosen to wear a bright red dress because that was Fizz all over, wasn't it? Daring as well as confident enough to pull off something so different. Her long, dark hair was hanging loose down her back and she looked gorgeous, Joe decided.

And *so* happy…

No wonder there was a collective sound like people were catching their breath around him. He thought he heard a happy sigh coming from Maggie, too.

Was *she* a believer as well? If she was, why hadn't she already conducted a successful husband hunt? She could have done it years ago and then she wouldn't have had to worry about the clock running out on her reproductive years. She wouldn't have had to even think about alternative routes to motherhood and she wouldn't have tried to involve *him* when bringing a child into the world was, without doubt, the last thing he would ever contemplate doing.

The celebrant welcomed everybody as the wail of the bagpipes finally faded.

'You have all been invited to attend today,' she told the gathering, 'because you are the family, friends and colleagues of Cooper and Fizz and they want you to witness their commitment to each other and share the joy of that promise.'

Joe sucked in a deep breath. He wasn't feeling particularly joyful right now. It was more than awkwardness filling that space between him and Maggie.

He was angry, that's what it was.

Or maybe it was more that he was sad. He let out that breath in a long sigh. He knew that Maggie had heard that sigh because he could feel the sideways glance he received. Turning his head just a fraction, he could catch a reflection of what he was feeling in her own eyes.

That hint of sadness.

There weren't that many things in life that you could be certain of and a true friendship was one of the most precious things there was. Maggie Lewis had been his favourite person to crew with ever since he'd joined the Aratika Rescue Base and the foundations of that trust between them had been rocked the other day. Possibly even damaged beyond repair judging by the aftershocks. All by a few words. There had been more than sadness in that swift glance they had just shared, however. An impression of something else was lingering. Regret? Along with a desire to put things right?

A flash of guilt threw itself into the confusing mix of emotions that was unsettling Joe right now. It wasn't as if Maggie had done anything wrong. After all, he'd been the one who'd thrown that anecdote of people using a friend as a sperm donor into the conversation. He just hadn't expected it to come back and bite him and it had only bitten that hard because it had touched a raw spot.

He'd overreacted, hadn't he?

Cooper and Fizz had written their own vows for this ceremony and the message that was coming through loud and clear was the deep friendship that was the basis of their relationship. The trust. How rare and special it was to find someone who felt the same way about you.

That was so true.

Not that Joe wanted to marry Maggie, of course. He had no desire to marry anybody. And he'd never been sexually attracted to her. He could acknowledge that she was a very attractive woman—she just wasn't his type. They had started out as colleagues and had become friends. Just because Cooper and Fizz had added benefits into their friendship that had taken them to a very different level didn't mean that his relationship with Maggie was any less valid.

All too often, in Joe's experience, friendships could outlast marriages.

As their friends exchanged a rather passionate kiss to seal their vows and the congregation clapped and cheered, Joe turned his head to find that Maggie was doing exactly the same thing and turning her head towards him.

This time, the smile they shared felt genuine.

The friendship was still there and there was an astonishing relief to be found in that knowledge. All they needed to do now was clear the air and sweep away the remnants of that disturbing suggestion of him helping her to achieve her dream of motherhood, and what better place to do that than during a party?

There were photographs against the dramatic backdrop of the cliffs and islands and a spectacular sunset. A live band was setting up for when they were going to provide the music for dancing later on and, in the meantime, there was a great range of wine and beer at the bar and delicious food that wasn't offered in any traditional kind of wedding breakfast. A spit roast was happening in the courtyard garden with an amazing range of vegetables or salads to accompany it and inside one of the reception rooms of the resort a taco station had been set up on a long trestle table.

'It's because we loved the taco nights at your place when Cooper was still living with you,' Fizz told Maggie.

'Yum…' Maggie had opened the lid of a huge container. 'That's proper pulled beef…'

'The taco shells are keeping warm as well.'

Harrison was already holding a shell and Laura was helping him to add shredded lettuce and grated cheese from the bowls further along the table.

'No tomatoes,' he told his mum. 'I hate tomatoes.'

'Sauce?'

'Only tomato sauce, not that hot stuff.'

Maggie laughed. 'But you just said you hated tomatoes, Harry.'

The deep voice right behind her after she spoke made her jump. It also made her heart skip a beat. Good grief…when had she ever been nervous to be in Joe's company before? But the way he'd looked at her when the ceremony had been getting underway—as if she'd done something completely unforgiveable—had made that tension between them feel like it was rapidly escalating. Mind you, the way he'd smiled at the end of the ceremony, when Fizz and Cooper were having their first kiss as husband and wife, had been a glimmer of hope. So was the amusement coating his words when he spoke now.

'Tomato sauce is different, Maggie. Everybody knows that.'

'Yeah.' Harrison nodded, although he'd edged closer to his mother. 'It doesn't even taste like tomatoes.'

'You can have whatever you want on your taco,' Fizz told him. 'They're the rules today.'

'And I get to stay up late, right?'

'Let's see how tired you get,' Laura cautioned. 'I don't want you feeling sick tomorrow.'

'I'm not going to get tired.' Harrison was looking determined. 'Because I know a secret about what's going to happen later and I have to be awake.'

'Oh?' Everybody turned to look at Fizz.

'Can't say.' She grinned. 'It's a secret. Harry only knows because he did so well with his special job today.' She glanced down at the wedding ring on her hand. 'And now I'm going to find a beer and make sure my husband has one, too. Enjoy the tacos, you lot.'

Joe was right behind Maggie as she loaded salad and cheese onto the meat in the crisp taco shell. They both added sliced jalapeño peppers and chilli sauce.

Drizzling the super-spicy sauce made Maggie smile. Instead of putting the bottle down again with the other condiments, she handed it to Joe.

'D'you remember the first time we ever worked together all those years ago?'

'When we knocked over the chilli sauce bottle on the table because we were both reaching for it at the same time?'

'And we discovered that there was someone else in the world who like putting hot sauce on scrambled eggs?'

The softening of Joe's features told Maggie that he was remembering more than those scrambled eggs. That it had been more than a moment of bonding as new colleagues. *The hotter the better* had become a private catchphrase and had ended up becoming a kind of code of encouragement. How many times had they been dispatched to what promised to be a challenging situation and they'd used that code?

This could get hot.

That's okay. That's the way we like it, remember?

Yeah...the hotter the better...

She could see the way Joe stilled for a moment, the sauce bottle still in his hands. Then he caught her gaze with the most direct look they'd shared since before that awkward conversation.

'It was the start of a great friendship,' he said quietly.

'One that I hope we still have,' Maggie said, just as softly. It was more than a great friendship, it was the best kind of friendship it was possible to have. She loved Joe and she knew that he felt the same way about her. It was a bond that nothing could break.

'I'm really sorry, Joe,' she added. 'I just wish I could wind the clock back and that I never talked to you about any of that baby stuff.'

'It wasn't entirely your fault. It was me who put the idea into your head.'

'It's not there now. Can we pretend it never happened?'

It seemed that Joe was thinking along the same lines.

'Consider it forgotten,' he said. 'Never to be discussed again.'

'What were we talking about?' Maggie tilted her head. 'I've forgotten.'

They both laughed, reaching for paper towels for what looked likely to be a messy meal, and virtually all of the tension that had been there between them seemed to evaporate with the sound of that laughter.

Normal service had been resumed and thank goodness for that. Maggie could finally relax enough to really enjoy this party to celebrate the wedding of two of her closest friends.

They couldn't really forget about it. Maggie knew that. Some things just couldn't be unheard in the same way that images from things seen could never be erased from your memory cells. But they could pretend to pretend, couldn't they? And maybe that would be enough to make everything all right again.

If nothing else, it was a good start.

CHAPTER THREE

THE SECRET THAT Harrison knew about was a fireworks display that happened later in the evening against the inky black sky over the cliff edge. Maggie used her phone camera to capture the excitement on the small boy's face as he watched the display from within the safe circle of his mother's arms. Then she turned to catch some of the amazing explosions of light and colour in the sky and, by chance, caught the moment when Fizz and Cooper—standing a little way in front of her—turned towards each other to steal a kiss.

They were only a silhouette against the bright display of exploding light in front of them but nobody could mistake the long hair being gently blown back from Fizz's head or the ruffled hem of Cooper's kilt. Maggie knew the instant she'd taken that photo that it was something special. The guests had all been firmly told that no wedding gifts other than their company were desired but Maggie now had the makings of the most perfect memento—just as good, if not possibly better than any of the formal photographs that had been taken today. She just needed to print this picture and find a pretty frame and she could present this captured moment of quintessential celebration when Cooper and Fizz came back from their honeymoon in Scotland.

Anticipating the pleasure of their reaction made her feel almost as good as it did to have her friendship with Joe back on track. It certainly made her feel confident enough to seek him out a little while later, after the fireworks had finished and the resort's four-wheel-drive taxis had taken the guests who needed to leave early back to the city.

She wanted to show someone the photo she was so proud of. Cooper and Fizz were out of the question, of course, and Laura had taken Harrison home because it was well past his bedtime already. There were plenty of people here who would love to see the romantic shot of the newly wed couple but there was only one person that Maggie really wanted to show it to and that was Joe.

Except that he was standing with Cooper, talking to the members of the band who were gearing up to try to get everybody on the dance floor for the rest of the evening.

'Bit of rock and roll, I reckon,' Cooper was saying as Maggie joined them. 'Nobody can resist that.'

'Like this?' The lead singer nodded to the others and they launched into Elvis Presley's 'Jailhouse Rock'.

The introductory notes were enough to bring a whoop from Fizz on the other side of the dance floor and Cooper had a huge grin on his face as he went to meet her in the middle of the space. Maggie's body was responding to the music without her even thinking about it, so when Joe grabbed her hand and pulled her onto the floor, she was only too happy to follow. She'd known that this new dress would be just perfect for a bit of rock and roll dancing with the way the skirts billowed as she was twirled and spun and even had her feet off the floor in a lift, but what she hadn't known was that Joe would be this good at it. One song led into another, the best music from the sixties and seventies that was far too good not to dance to, and it wasn't until quite some time later that Maggie was breathless and tired enough to head off the dance floor for a rest. Joe seemed happy to follow her.

'Where on earth did you learn to dance like that?'

Joe shrugged. 'Got dragged along to lessons once with a girlfriend.'

'Takes more than a few lessons to learn that many moves.'

He grinned. 'Guess she lasted a bit longer than most. In fact, she was the one I was with when we first met and she lasted almost as long as you and Richard, from what I remember. Maybe that was because she was more interested in dancing than anything off-putting like getting married or having babies.'

Maggie froze for a moment at the reminder of what she'd managed to forget about completely while they'd been dancing. But Joe was still smiling.

'Want a drink?'

'I need about a gallon of water, I think.'

'I need a very cold lager. And a bit of fresh air, maybe? Don't know about you but I'm cooking after all that exercise.'

'It was great fun, though.' Maggie followed Joe outside when they both had a drink in their hands. 'I really should get back into doing some dancing on a regular basis. It was always my exercise of choice.'

Joe shook his head. 'Not for me. You can't beat windsurfing. And Wellington's perfect for it.'

'Mmm… I was going to say that there's always some wind here but…look at this…' Maggie held her palm up above her head. 'There's not even a puff right now. What a perfect evening.'

There were bench seats built into the outside of the low stone wall surrounding the courtyard that provided the same view of the cliff edge that the wedding guests had been treated to earlier and, by tacit consent, Maggie and Joe headed for one of them and sat down. The white chairs had all been cleared away but the pretty archway was still in place and, above it, a crescent moon hung in the night sky.

'I've got to get a photo of that.' Maggie put her glass down on the bench beside her and fished in her pocket for her phone. As soon as she'd caught the image, she remembered the earlier shot and held her phone out to Joe.

'Look at this.'

'Wow…that's very cool. Looks like a cover for a romance novel.'

'They'll love it, won't they? I thought I'd

get it framed while they're away on honeymoon.'

'They're not calling it a honeymoon, remember? It's been a huge thing for Fizz to even get married again and Cooper said he was careful to call this holiday a "babymoon". He wants to show her his home country before she's too pregnant to be allowed to fly long-haul.'

Maggie sighed. 'I'd almost forgotten the tragedy of her last honeymoon. Maybe because she's looked so incredibly happy today.'

'They both have, haven't they? Good luck to them, too. I hope they stay that way for ever.'

They sat in silence for a long moment, staring up at the moon.

Maggie took a sip of her champagne, a kaleidoscope of images from today's ceremony flashing through her mind. She loved weddings but the aftermath did tend to make her feel a bit lonely these days. Kind of like the way dealing with babies or even talking about them could make her arms feel empty. She slid a sideways glance at Joe.

'Have you ever got close to getting married, Joe?' she asked. 'You've never been short of female company in the time I've known you. Except for now, mind you. What happened to the last one…what's her name? That redheaded nurse?'

'Amanda.' Joe took a swig of his beer. 'I was a rebound. She went back to her ex and got engaged to him.' He wiped his mouth with the back of his hand and returned the curious glance. 'What about you? Why are you still single? Especially given that you like the idea of having kids so much.'

Maggie shrugged, aware that he'd avoided answering her question by turning the tables, but she wasn't going to force him to talk about something he preferred to keep private.

'Just haven't found the right person, I guess,' she said. 'And I'm not about to settle for anything less than the "real thing".'

Joe's breath came out in a dismissive huff. 'You don't really believe in that, do you?'

'In love? Of course I do. How can you even ask that when you can see how happy Cooper and Fizz are?'

'I mean that idea that there's one perfect person out there and when you find them you're destined to live happily-ever-after. That whole romantic myth of the "real thing".' He took another swig of his drink. 'Yes, it can work. Sometimes. If you're really lucky but, all too often, it turns into a disaster. That's the real reason I'm still single,' he added. 'It's because I don't believe in it. In any of it.'

Maggie's jaw dropped as she caught a note of something like bitterness in his tone. 'Don't let anyone else hear you say that tonight. Man…talk about raining on someone's parade.'

Joe made an apologetic face. 'You're right. Okay… I won't say anything else. And, for the record, I think that Cooper and Fizz make a great couple. If anyone can make it work, those two can.'

Maggie couldn't help trying to score another point. 'Maybe that's because they've found the "real thing".'

The sound Joe made now sounded resigned. 'Which is what, exactly?'

Maggie considered the question. She'd asked herself often enough when past relationships had failed for one reason or another.

'It's got friendship in there,' she answered. 'It needs a solid foundation of genuine friendship. Just being able to enjoy each other's company and respect each other's opinions.'

'We're friends,' Joe said. 'But it's never going to be anything more than that.'

'God, no,' Maggie agreed. 'That's because there's no chemistry. Just being friends is never going to be enough. I found that out with Richard. You've got to be attracted to someone to fall in love with them. Really, really attracted. And it happens instantly, if it's real.'

'That's just hormones. It wears off.'

'Probably. But if it lasts long enough for a friendship to develop as well it can create something that *will* last. For some people it lasts their whole lives. My parents are like that and that's what I want to find. They fell in love at first sight and it's still there. They're in their sixties and they still hold hands when they're walking down the street. They still look at each other sometimes in a way that makes me want to tell them to get a room.'

'Good luck with that,' Joe muttered. 'At least you won't be getting married just because you're having a baby. Much better to do that by yourself if that's what you really want. Better for everybody but especially better for the kid.'

This time, something in his tone struck a note that made Maggie think there was more to his words than what was on the surface. It took her back to that look of horror on his face when he'd realised she was thinking of him as a potential baby daddy and she knew, instinctively, that it was the cause of how awkward it had felt between them afterwards. Maybe it also had something to do with that bitterness that had crept into his voice when he'd said he didn't believe in true love.

As Joe had reminded her, they were good friends. And friends cared, didn't they, when they learned about things that could affect their quality of life?

'What makes you say that?' she asked gently.

'Kids get caught in the flak,' Joe said quietly. 'They can grow up thinking that it's their fault. That, no matter how hard they try, they can never fix things.'

Maggie blinked. Yep…there was something deep and dark beneath those words. She'd never thought of her tall, confident, outgoing crew partner as a small child who might have had a less than happy upbringing but right now she wanted to find that little boy and give him a cuddle. To tell him that things were going to be okay one day.

The best she could do, however, was to

simply sit there beside him and offer a sympathetic ear and encouragement to talk about it if that was what he wanted.

'You're talking from personal experience?'

Joe drained his glass. 'Yep. I was that kid.'

Maggie swallowed hard. 'I'm so sorry, Joe... Didn't anybody try and help you?'

The slow shake of his head was heartbreaking. 'From the outside, I doubt that anybody even guessed. My mother got pregnant, so my father did "the decent thing" and married her. Maybe they believed it might work out okay in the end but it didn't. He walked out when I was about five and my mother never stopped telling me that it was my fault. That I was an accident. That he hadn't wanted a kid and she was far too young and hadn't had the chance to get a good job or meet someone special. Bottom line was that I'd ruined her life.'

'She *told* you that? When you were so little? That's...' Maggie shook her head with disbelief. 'That's just awful...'

'She apologised for it later. She met someone else eventually and I think she's happy enough but it was more than enough to put me off the whole business of marriage and kids.'

Maggie was almost cringing. 'And then I go and start talking about sperm donors and baby daddies. I'm really sorry, Joe.'

'It's me that should apologise. You're right. I'm raining on the parade here. I don't know why I even told you any of that crap.'

Maggie did. There was an apology of some kind hidden in there, for how he'd reacted the other day.

'If I'd known,' she told him, 'I would never have started that conversation. Not in a million years.'

'What conversation?' Joe flashed her a grin and the glimpse of that unhappy little boy faded away. 'I can't remember any of it.' He got to his feet. 'They're playing my song in there. You coming in or do I have to go and find a new dance partner?'

Maggie felt a sudden need to shake off anything negative to do with weddings and babies. She wanted to be happy for her friends and she did, genuinely, believe that Cooper and Fizz were perfect for each other and that they were going to be happy together.

And maybe it hadn't been the best time for Joe to tell her about his unhappy history but there'd been a reason for that, hadn't there? He was offering her an explanation of why she had shocked him so badly and it was enough of an apology for her to believe that they could really put that conversation behind them. By the time they were working together again, it would all be forgiven and forgotten.

'Wait for me...' Maggie jumped to her feet to follow Joe. 'That's actually *my* song, not yours...'

Why on earth had he told Maggie so much about his childhood?

Joe closed his locker door and headed upstairs.

'You're an early bird.' Shirley was busy in the kitchen area of the staffroom. 'There's been a couple of late calls so the night shift crews aren't back yet.'

Joe glanced at his watch. He was very early. He'd woken up feeling an echo of the tension that had been between himself and Maggie when he'd arrived at the wedding two days ago and he couldn't just lie there and think about it. He'd needed to get up and get moving but even a run hadn't quite dealt with that note of tension.

He had ended the night of the wedding feeling like he and Maggie had not only mended any crack in their friendship but had strengthened its foundations considerably, but that had been flavoured by a party atmosphere of music and fun and a few beers. How different was it going to be when they were working together again? Now that Maggie knew something about him that nobody else did?

'I could smell those sausages,' Joe told Shirley. 'It was irresistible.'

Shirley smile was delighted. 'We've got bacon as well. And I'm going to grill tomatoes. Want a piece of toast while you're waiting?'

'No, thanks, Shirley. I won't spoil my appetite for one of your awesome breakfasts. I'll have a coffee and read the paper.'

He sat down at the table but he was reading headlines without taking much notice because he was still wondering whether his working relationship with Maggie might have changed after telling her something so personal.

Joe had never told anyone about how unhappy his childhood had been. He didn't even think about it, if he could help it. It was past history. Okay, it had shaped the way he lived his life now but why he might not want to get married was his own business. He was quite happy for other people to see him as being so committed to his career he didn't have the time or inclination to complicate his personal life by having his own family. He knew that some people considered him to be self-centred by making his life all about himself—his career, his hobbies, his parade of female companions—but he'd never cared about that, either.

Until Maggie had asked him to father a baby for her.

Until—for a split second—he'd actually imagined the reality of that. Of Maggie becoming pregnant. Of him feeling the pressure of being forced to do the 'decent' thing, even if that meant being involved in a child's life rather than marrying the mother. Of another child in the world who could end up without a father or feeling like his existence was some kind of horrible mistake.

'And here's another early bird.' Shirley's voice cut through his thoughts. 'Don't tell me you could smell the sausages halfway across town, too, Maggie?'

Joe's gaze flicked up and caught Maggie's instantly. Was she arriving at work early due to the same hint of nerves that had been bothering him? If so, it didn't show. Maggie looked just the same as ever, with that ready smile and palpable eagerness for whatever challenges lay ahead that day. She was one of those people who could brighten a room simply by walking into it.

'Morning, Shirley.' Maggie went to give their volunteer housekeeper a hug. 'How are your feet after all the dancing the other evening?'

Shirley sighed happily. 'Wasn't it just the best wedding ever?'

'It was. I haven't had so much fun in a very long time.'

'You and Joe were the stars of the dance floor,' Shirley said. 'Everybody knew that you could dance, Maggie, but Joe surprised us all.'

'I know. Talk about hidden talents… Who knows what else he's hiding? Maybe he's good at knitting?'

Both women laughed and then Maggie's smile was being directed at Joe and he found himself releasing a breath he hadn't known he was holding.

That was why he'd told her something so private the other night. Because he wanted her to understand why he could never do something like casually fathering a baby. Because he didn't want her to think he was being selfish or that he didn't value their friendship. Because he didn't want the 'dream team' to break apart.

Now he could relax. It was all good. Neither confessing something so personal about his childhood nor the step Maggie had taken onto totally unwelcome territory with the sperm donor conversation mattered any longer. Nothing had changed.

'Just wait till Christmas,' he warned them. 'You'll be first on the list for my homemade knitted slippers.'

Nothing had changed.

So why did it still feel like something *had* changed?

Responding swiftly to their first helicopter callout that day, getting airborne and getting as much information as possible about the scenario they were heading into was the same as it always was.

'Twenty-six-year-old male. Fall from height.' Joe read his pager message aloud as he got himself into the kind of head space he needed to be when heading towards a potentially major trauma.

'What height?' Nick, the crewman, sounded curious.

'Not clear,' Maggie put in. 'He was putting up scaffolding on a high level of an industrial building but nobody actually saw that he was falling until he bounced off a platform about three metres off the ground.'

'Landed on concrete?'

'Yep.'

'Ouch…'

'You said it.' Joe was thinking of just how serious this could be. A major head injury, serious fractures, chest trauma. Would their patient still be alive by the time they got on site?

He was not only alive, he was conscious.

Maggie got to the man's side first, although they hadn't had any discussion about who was going to lead this case. Not that it mattered and that was something that hadn't changed, either.

'Hey, Sean… I'm Maggie and this is my partner, Joe. We heard you had a bit of a fall…'

The young man groaned. 'It hurts really bad,' he told Maggie.

'Where does it hurt the most?'

'Legs…belly…'

'Were you knocked out?'

'Dunno…'

'He was out of it for a few minutes.' One of the group of builders clustered around the injured man was keen to help Maggie get the answers she needed. 'But he was breathing okay. We knew he wasn't dead.'

'And we didn't move him,' another man told her. 'We knew he might have hurt his back.'

'Good work.' Maggie nodded.

Joe glanced up from where he was getting a set of vital signs. Sean's airway was clear and his breathing was rapid but not shallow enough to suggest a serious chest injury. His heart rate was up and his skin was pale and clammy, which made it more likely that he was losing blood from somewhere and going into shock. Joe was reaching for the IV roll to get a line in and some fluids started when he glanced up at the circle of men around them and noticed that every set of male eyes here was focussed on Maggie.

Because she was leading the assessment of their workmate?

Or was it because she was blonde and cute?

And there it was. *Bang.* The 'something' that had changed. Not that he was going to spend more than a split second to take the information on board right now but he was aware of it.

He was thinking of Maggie as more than his paramedic partner. A part of his brain had stepped back to give him a bigger picture and he was observing her as a woman. As a potential mother. Or wife, perhaps, if she got over being so picky about trying to find the non-existent perfect man. For heaven's sake, she clearly had no trouble attracting male attention.

'I'll get some fluids up,' he muttered.

Maggie nodded. She was into her secondary survey now, having checked that there was no visible major bleeding going on.

'No external sign of head injury.'

'He had his hard hat on,' someone told them. 'But he pulled it off as soon as he woke up.'

'Ow...' Sean's cry was almost a scream as Maggie's hands reached his lower abdomen.

'Is that pain in your tummy? Here?'

'No…it's in my back…my legs… *Ow...*'

'He's got outward rotation of his left foot.' Joe finished securing the IV line he'd just put in. 'Hip or pelvic fracture?'

'And/or femoral. He's in a lot of pain.'

'Fentanyl and ketamine?' As usual, the lines of who was the lead medic in this case were blurring. They were well into their 'dream team' zone, where they could work as a single unit that had the advantage of two brains and two pairs of skilled hands.

'Please. I'll get a collar on. And a SAM?'
Joe nodded his agreement.

The SAM was a pelvic splint, a wide belt that Maggie slid beneath the hollow in Sean's lower back so that Joe could catch the strap on the end and help her position it low on Sean's hips.

'Hang on a tick… I haven't checked his pockets for anything like keys.'

Maggie double-checked the pockets on the other side. 'Clear.'

'Same.' Joe fed the long strap through the buckle on the belt and then applied tension on his side as Maggie pulled on a loop on the other side of the buckle. The belt tightened until it clicked into a locked position.

They had pain relief on board for their patient, oxygen and fluids running, and a neck collar as well as the pelvic splint. They still needed to get him securely onto their stretcher with his neck further protected by the cushions and straps that would prevent his head moving and then get him into an emergency department as quickly as possible where he could get the scans that would reveal any injuries and the surgery that was highly likely to be needed.

It wasn't until a long time later that they had the opportunity to do what they always tried to do after a scene like that, which was to think about the job as a whole, tick off the things they had done well and to discuss anything that they thought could have been managed better.

Except that when Joe took that mental step back to look at the job as a whole, he found he was still looking at Maggie in that different way.

'Ooh, look…' Maggie had opened the fridge in the staffroom kitchen. 'There's some left-over sausages from breakfast. Fancy one rolled up in a slice of bread with some tomato sauce?'

'Make that chilli sauce and I'm in.'

'Oh, *great* idea…' Maggie's grin was as good as applause. 'You're not just a pretty face, are you, Joe?' Her grin widened as she straightened, a container of sausages in her hands. 'Oh, that's right…you're actually not a pretty face at all.'

Maggie was, though. From this new and speculative viewpoint, as he watched her ferry the supplies they needed to the big table, Joe was rating his colleague as if he were a man who was seeing her for the first time—like those men on the building site this morning. Petite in height but a bit curvy in all the right places, blonde curls that refused to be restrained in any meaningful manner and big, blue eyes. Joe had never actually realised quite how blue they were until he'd seen her wearing that dress at the wedding the other day.

What was wrong with him that he'd never been attracted to his partner? Or *had* he been attracted when he'd first met Maggie and simply put it into the 'off limits' basket because they had both been in long-term relationships at the time? No, it had to be a chemistry thing, like Maggie had suggested, because from this viewpoint he'd give her a ten out of ten on an average male's attractiveness ratings chart. He also had the advantage of knowing how smart she was. How skilled. How kind she was to animals and small children. She'd be the perfect wife—for someone who wanted to be part of a big family.

Joe picked up a slice of bread, buttered it, put a sausage in the middle and slathered it with chilli sauce before rolling it up and taking a big bite.

'Mmm…'

Maggie made the same full-mouth mumbling noise of pleasure and Joe caught her gaze.

And then it really hit him…

He wasn't just thinking about Maggie in general terms of her attractiveness and why she was still single.

A very deep part of his brain was thinking about her in a much more specific way. Joe dragged his gaze free of Maggie's so fast it had to be impossible for her to have guessed what was going through his head. He certainly hoped that was the case, anyway, because he couldn't quite believe what it was he was thinking about.

If he'd been open to her crazy idea about finding a baby daddy, how would it have played out?

With an impersonal sample bottle and a turkey baster? Or would Maggie have thought a more natural form of conception might have been preferable? Maybe it had been the sound she'd made expressing her pleasure in the food she had in her mouth that had been the catalyst for going down this particular track. Joe could hear an echo of it again. It was just the kind of sound he could imagine her making in bed, if she was really enjoying some company…

Oh…*man*… He suddenly found it too much of a challenge to swallow the mouthful of food he had finished chewing. Maybe it wasn't a part of his brain that was responsible for what had changed between Maggie and himself.

At this precise moment, it felt like it was a deep part of his body that had been shocked into life by the whole episode of having to think about Maggie and baby-making. And it was putting two and two together and coming up with a total that was as unexpected as it was inappropriate. It felt like some sort of chemical reaction was taking place and it was…appalling…

Forcing himself to swallow was actually painful. Slamming both mental and physical doors to what was going on in his head and his body was also almost painful but it had to be done. Quickly and conclusively. And it could never be allowed to happen again.

Ever.

'I think you used too much sauce,' Maggie told him. 'You look like you're breaking out in a sweat.'

'Doubt it.' Joe didn't dare look up to catch her gaze again. Instead, he took another bite of his sausage and, this time, it was much easier to swallow.

Maggie wasn't to know that anything had changed between them so all he had to do was pretend things were normal and they would be again. Hopefully very soon.

He could do this.

No sweat.

CHAPTER FOUR

'HE'S GOING TO make a great dad, one day, isn't he?'

For a moment, Maggie couldn't think of anything to say in response to Laura's comment, so she turned her head to see what had prompted it.

Harrison was a little way away from where she and Laura were unpacking the barbecue supplies onto one of the picnic tables at this beach, watching Joe set up his windsurfing board and sail.

'What's that?' she heard Harrison ask.

'It's called an up-haul. It's a rope for pulling the sail up out of the water.'

'And what's that?'

'That's called a dagger board. It's like a big fin. If I pull on this lever here, it makes the board go down, see?'

'Why?'

'You can use it to stop the board being so wobbly sometimes. To stabilise it.'

'Can I try?'

'To pull the lever? Sure.'

'No…' Harrison looked up at Joe. 'Can I try in the water—like Jack's going to do?'

'Sorry, buddy…you'd need a wetsuit in this cold water. And you're a bit little to try windsurfing just yet. The sail's quite heavy to pull up.'

Jack was zipping up the back of his wetsuit as he joined Joe and Harrison. 'I don't know if *I'm* going to be able to do it, Harry,' he said. 'This is the first time I've ever tried windsurfing. You just wait. I bet I fall into the water with a big splash.'

Harrison laughed and Joe ruffled his hair, which made the small boy duck his head shyly. 'You can help me,' he told Harry. 'I'm going to stand here and tell Jack what to do. You can watch and tell me if you think he's doing a good job, okay?'

'Okay.' Harrison's nod was solemn. He was going to take this responsibility seriously.

Maggie was smiling as she turned back to Laura. 'He's so cute.'

'Which one? Jack, Joe or Harry?'

'Harry, of course.'

'Yeah…' Laura's smile was misty. 'He is pretty cute, isn't he?'

She seemed to have forgotten the comment she'd made about Joe's future as a father and Maggie certainly wasn't going to remind her. She'd never reveal the private information that Joe had shared with her about not wanting to be a husband or father and she would never, ever break that confidence and tell anyone about why he felt like that. It felt good to know that he'd trusted her enough to tell her and even better that she could protect his privacy. Their friendship was back on track. Better than ever, even, judging by the last few shifts they had worked together.

'It's a treat to get out like this to a beach,' Laura added. 'How often do we get a day like this on a weekend?'

'About as often as we all get a day off at the same time.'

'I know, right? When Jack said that Joe was going to give him a windsurfing lesson, I knew we had to gatecrash the party. That's why I offered to do the barbecue.'

'And I wasn't going to miss out on the fun.' Maggie nodded. She lifted the lid of a cooler. 'Did we remember to put bacon in here? It's not a proper barbecue without bacon.'

'We've got hamburgers, bacon and some steak. There's wine and beer in the other cooler. Ooh…why don't we take a break and have a glass of wine while we watch the boys?'

'Sounds like a plan.'

By the time Joe had shown Jack how to carry the board and sail into water that was deep enough for him to try getting on, Laura and Maggie were set up on the sand, sipping their drinks and waiting for the entertainment.

'Okay, Jack…' Joe called. 'Make sure the dagger board is down and that you're standing in line with the sail on the other side with the wind at your back.'

'Yep. All good,' Jack called back.

'Now put your hands on the centre line, shoulder-width apart and climb onto the board.'

'He's making it wobble,' Harrison said.

'He is,' Joe agreed. 'Stay on your knees, Jack. And hold onto the up-haul before you try standing up.'

'Doesn't look that easy,' Laura said to Maggie.

'No… Uh-oh…'

Trying to lift the sail, Jack was leaning too far back. He lost his balance and crashed

ALISON ROBERTS **89**

back into the water with a huge splash that make Harrison shriek with laughter. Laura's chuckle was an echo of her son's enjoyment.

'It's so good to see him out like this. He used to be so scared of men.'

'I know. I remember when Jack moved in with us and Harry burst into tears every time he came into the room.'

'He never had a problem with Cooper, though, which surprised me because Cooper's so big.'

'He likes Joe now, too.' Maggie was looking at the backs of the two figures in front of them. Tall Joe and short Harry. Their postures were almost identical, standing there with their feet apart and their arms folded. It gave her a beat of something rather poignant because it looked as though they could be a father and son. Because Laura had been right in that Joe would make a great father. He was always so kind and gentle in dealing with children but he could be firm if he needed to be— —to keep them safe or provide essential medical treatment.

It was completely a personal choice whether or not to be a parent but it was sad to think that no child would get to have Joe as a father. And that he might miss out on learning that a family could be so much better than the one he'd experienced as a child himself.

'We're lucky,' Laura said. 'It was the best decision I ever made to move into a big house and find people to share it with rather than to stay by myself with Harry in that small apartment. He'd never have had any male role models if I'd done that.'

That was probably true, Maggie thought. She'd never known Laura to show the slightest interest in dating anybody and she never talked about Harrison's father.

'It can't be easy, being a single mum.'

'No.' Laura took another sip of her wine. 'But it's much better than being in a bad situation with a partner.'

Maggie made a sympathetic sound. She'd always had the impression that Laura had escaped from an abusive relationship but she'd never tried asking questions that her flatmate might not want to answer. Given her own recent thoughts about choosing to be a single mother, though, she was curious.

'How old was Harry when you split up with his father?'

'About three months. Just when I was due to go back to work after maternity leave.'

'Oh, no…what did you do?'

'What could I do? I just did my best and

got on with it. I'd already arranged childcare so that I could go back to work.'

'So you were working all day and then looking after a tiny baby by yourself all night...'

'It wasn't easy,' Laura agreed. 'Leaving him in day care when he was so little was the hardest thing I'd ever done but we muddled through somehow. And life's good now. I love my job and Harry's happy. What more could I want?'

Again, Maggie responded with no more than a sound of agreement. She was answering that question silently, however. Maybe Laura could want a partner to share the parenting. Or to make part of her life about herself as someone special and not about her being a mother or a nurse. Even with a child as company constantly out of work hours and adult flatmates around a lot of the time, there had to be moments when Laura felt lonely or that there was something missing in her life.

The way Maggie did at weddings?

Or when she was holding other people's babies?

How much worse could that be, though, if she was struggling to hold down her job and look after a baby alone, the way Laura had done?

'I don't think I could do it,' she murmured aloud.

'What—windsurfing?' Laura was watching Jack again.

'Keep your hands on the boom,' Joe was telling him. 'You lean the sail towards the back of the board to turn into the wind and to the nose of the board to turn away from the wind.'

'He's wobbling again,' Harrison shouted.

'He's okay. Look at that. Well done, Jack…'

'You could do that with your hands tied behind your back,' Laura told Maggie. 'You can ride a motorbike, for heaven's sake. And dangle out of helicopters when you need to. You could do anything you put your mind to.'

'I was talking about being a single mother. I was actually thinking of trying it, seeing as I can't seem to find anyone remotely suitable to partner up with.'

'Really?' Laura sounded shocked. 'How was that going to work? Get pregnant and not let the guy know?'

'No, I'd never do that. But you know… there are sperm banks available.'

Laura shook her head. 'Don't rush into anything. I mean… I love Harry to bits and I wouldn't be without him but it's not what I would have deliberately chosen for my life. No way... You've still got lots of time to find someone.'

The sound Maggie made this time was less than convinced.

'It does happen. Look at Cooper and Fizz.'

'They're due back from their honeymoon soon, aren't they?'

'Next week. I'm looking forward to having Fizz back working in Emergency.' Laura scrambled to her feet. 'Looks like Jack's had enough of his first lesson. Might be time to get that barbecue started.'

But Maggie stayed where she was for the moment. Joe had taken the board from Jack and was heading further out to sea, making it look easy as he manoeuvred the sail to catch the wind and began to pick up speed.

Jack and Harrison came past where Maggie was sitting on the sand.

'That's a lot harder than it looks,' he told her. 'The way my shoulders feel right now, I might have trouble lifting a beer.'

'You wobbled a lot,' Harrison agreed. 'But Joe said you did a good job.' He skipped ahead of Jack. 'Mum? I'm *starving*...'

Maggie was still watching Joe, who was skimming across the relatively flat water at an impressive speed now. He was making the board jump from the surface, catching a short ride in the air before landing again and doing turns that changed his direction so swiftly and smoothly it looked like a kind of dance. She knew how much muscle strength that would take. Like other forms of dancing, being able to make it look that effortless and elegant actually took enormous strength and skill.

And that made Maggie remember all the dancing they'd done at Cooper and Fizz's wedding and how much fun it had been. She could almost feel his arms around her and the strength she had felt in his muscles as he'd lifted her feet off the ground and spun her around. And then, somehow, her memories and what she was watching right now and even that conversation with Laura somehow coalesced in Maggie's brain, and she was simultaneously thinking about Joe not wanting to be a father and what he'd looked like standing beside Harrison and about his muscles and his arms around her and even the disappointment of knowing that he would never agree to be a sperm donor crept into the mix, and the alchemy of it all became very weird.

Because Maggie suddenly thought about what might have happened if Joe had been open to the idea of fathering a baby for her and how they might have achieved her goal. For the first time ever, she was thinking of Joe…and sex…and it was doing something very peculiar deep inside her body. She knew what that spear of sensation was all about, too.

Physical attraction.

Pure, unadulterated lust, that's what it was.

Her body liked the idea of having sex with Joe. A lot. So much so that Maggie could feel the flush of colour heating her cheeks and she had to scramble to her feet and turn her back on Joe before he carried his board and sail from the water and got close enough to see what might be a very odd expression on her face.

She had to get her head straight and make sure she never tapped into that line of thought again. Not that it had anything to do with any plan of becoming a single mother that had been fading away even before she'd taken Laura's warning on board. No…it was bad enough feeling any kind of attraction to a good friend. Not only a good friend but the person she loved working with so much. The other half of the 'dream team'.

If Joe knew that she had entertained any

thoughts of sexual attraction to him, he'd either be horrified and back off to a safe space or he might be curious enough to make something happen. Either way, it would not only change and potentially destroy the friendship they had, it could do exactly the same thing to their working relationship.

No matter how good that sex would probably be, it wouldn't be worth it. Maggie was going to make absolutely sure that nobody knew what she'd been thinking. She wasn't even going to allow herself to think about it again.

Ever…

Thoughts could be like unwanted seeds. Weeds that insisted on growing no matter how diligently you tried to pull them out.

Despite Joe's best efforts, it was proving impossible to stop having inappropriate thoughts about Maggie. Even in a moment like this, when he should have been revelling in what was a different kind of adventure at work. Getting a callout to assist the coastguard in responding to a medical event on a ship was the kind of variety that made their job so exciting and Maggie was clearly loving every minute of this wild ride out to the entrance of Wellington Harbour. Daylight was fading and the winds were strong enough to have made the prospect of winching a paramedic onto a boat too dangerous so here they were cresting huge swells and crashing into troughs in this powerful and well-equipped rescue vessel. Maggie was small and light enough to be bounced right out of her seat and she was hanging on tightly as a splash of spray caught her face, but she was laughing as she shook the sea water from her skin.

And, okay, the rigid-hulled inflatable boat was unsinkable with the fat air cushions surrounding it but most people would be terrified by being thrown around in waves this big. Nothing really scared Maggie, did it? Or, if it did, she kept it well hidden.

Who knew how sexy that kind of courage in a woman could be?

Just how physically attractive his colleague was had been right under his nose for so long but it was only now that the genie had been released from the bottle that it was becoming apparent that there had been a lot of other stuff bottled up as well.

Like the way Maggie looked when she was in her leather gear for riding her bike.

Or the way she'd looked on the beach that night, when they had been toasting marshmallows on a driftwood fire after he'd given Jack his first windsurfing lesson. The way her face had glowed in the firelight. The sound of her laughter. Although focussing on Maggie had perhaps been a way to distract himself from the poignant feeling of loss that having Harrison standing beside him and 'helping' as he'd watched Jack's progress. He'd felt an odd bond with the little boy who didn't have a father around but at least Laura would never make Harry feel like he'd ruined her life. He was clearly the centre of his mother's universe and deeply loved. A little boy as lucky as all children deserved to be.

'*Whoa...*'

They hit the bottom of the next swell with a thump that sent Maggie toppling sideways. Both Joe and one of the coastguard crew reached to help her catch her balance but Joe got there first. For a moment, as he helped her upright, his face was within inches of hers.

'You okay?'

'I'm good.' Maggie was smiling and nodding but then her gaze caught Joe's as she settled back into her seat and he saw the flare of...*something*...

Oh, no... Had she guessed what had just

gone through his head? When their faces had
been so close? That they had been almost
close enough to kiss…?

He knew exactly how horrified she would
be if that was the case. He could still hear
the echoes of that conversation they'd had at
Cooper and Fizz's wedding about what Maggie thought the 'real thing' was all about and
he'd said that he and Maggie were friends but
it would never be anything more than that
and Maggie's response had been vehement.

God, no…because there's no chemistry.

What he was feeling right now felt a lot
like rather powerful chemistry but he knew
it was one-sided.

He had to try harder, that was all there
was to it.

Good grief…

Had she really thought that she could
simply order herself to stop thinking about
something and have it magically disappear
from her head?

Ever since that trip to the beach, Maggie
had found it impossible to stop those inappropriate thoughts about Joe from sneaking
into her head. Or sometimes into her body
before her head. Like the way they just had
when she'd felt his hands grabbing onto her

body to stop her falling. Catching his gaze had been a big mistake because that had only made it worse. Hazel brown eyes had always been her favourite colour so how come she'd never noticed that Joe had eyes that looked like there was sunshine making the brown so golden and warm.

It had felt like it took far too much time to drag her gaze clear of his and, for a horrible micro-second, Maggie wondered if he'd guessed what she'd been feeling and thinking. She clung onto the handles on the edge of her seat even more tightly as they rode the next swell. Falling into Joe's arms again would not be a good idea.

Catching his gaze like that again was a no-no, too. Imagine if he knew what she was thinking? He'd spelled out his lack of interest in anything more than friendship the night they'd been talking at the wedding when he'd said that they would never be more than friends. And she'd been so quick and definite in her agreement, hadn't she?

How could things have changed so much?

It was a puzzle that Maggie didn't even want to think about and it was more than easy enough to forget thanks to the adrenaline rush of this job. The ride on the rough sea was awesome but the challenge of getting alongside the larger fishing vessel, catching the ladder that swung against the hull and getting themselves and their equipment in through the narrow door needed absolute concentration. That they completed that part of this challenge successfully was enough to have Maggie grinning from ear to ear as Joe and some of the ship's crew helped to pull her inside and out of the wind.

'Well done. That wasn't easy.'

The fishermen were grinning back at her but Joe wasn't. He almost looked irritated as he picked up one end of the stretcher that had their pack strapped onto it.

'Let's go. Where's our patient?'

'Follow us. He's going to be happy to see you guys. He's in a hell of a lot of pain.'

'He's had a fall, yes?'

'Yeah. He lost his footing on a ladder and he was hanging on with one arm but then he fell when we hit another wave. Looks like he's broken something. His arm, or his shoulder, maybe.'

There was a strong smell of fish on this lower deck of the ship and it was rolling enough to make the combination a little nauseating. Maggie breathed through her mouth to lessen the impact.

'Did he get knocked out?' she asked.

'Don't think so. Not judging by the amount of noise he was making as soon as it happened, anyway. Listen…that's him you can hear now.'

Fishermen were tough but a complete dislocation and possible fracture of an elbow joint was a very painful injury. It was also urgent that it be relocated as quickly as possible because of the danger of damage to the brachial artery and nerves.

'Hang in there, mate,' Joe told him, as soon as he'd introduced himself and Maggie. 'We're going to get some pain relief on board for you asap and try and sort that elbow out for you. Are you allergic to anything that you know of?'

The injured man, who had turned out to be the ship's chef, shook his head. Even that movement made him cry out in pain as he tried to hold his arm still.

Maggie busied herself getting an IV line established as Joe quickly checked the man for any other major injuries and then looked at his limb baselines on the injured arm.

'Sharp scratch,' she warned, when she was about to slide the cannula into their patient's skin. 'Don't move…'

With the level of pain the chef was already

in, he didn't even notice the needle going into his arm.

'Can you wiggle your fingers for me?' Joe asked. 'If you close your eyes, can you feel me touching your hand here? And here?'

'Limb baselines are down,' Joe told Maggie moments later as she was drawing up the drugs she knew they were going to need. 'Skin's cold, capillary refill is slow and I can only get a faint radial pulse.'

'I'll get set up for oxygen and SpO2 monitoring.' Maggie reached for the ECG dots for the life pack and a mask for the oxygen cylinder.

Joe administered the drugs that would sedate their patient deeply enough to make it possible to try and relocate his elbow and then he and Maggie positioned themselves, with Maggie wrapping her hands around his forearm and Joe preparing to provide countertraction on the upper arm.

'Ready?'

Maggie caught his gaze. 'Ready.'

How often had they done this? she mused as they gently began to apply pressure in opposite directions. Worked like this, so closely together, knowing that each of them completely trusted the other. If she was ever sick or injured, Maggie thought, it would be Joe she would want to turn up and look after her. She would trust him with her life, if it ever came to that.

Joe held her gaze for a moment longer.

'Even if this doesn't work,' Joe said, 'it should restore circulation enough to be helpful.'

His crew stood in the background, watching.

'It's still hurting him, isn't it?' one of them muttered.

'He won't remember it,' Joe told them. 'And…there we go. I think we've got it in the right place now. We're going to splint the arm and get him secured onto our stretcher there. We might need a bit of help from you guys to get him onto the coastguard boat.'

'Wind's dropping,' someone told them. 'It won't be quite as bad as it was when you got here.'

It was still a mission. Climbing down that ladder, after the stretcher had been lowered and taken on board, was the scariest thing Maggie had done in a very long time. It didn't help that a wave broke and soaked her as she reached the lower rungs. With salt water in her eyes and a boat that was a moving target, she was extremely grateful to feel several hands grabbing her arms to pull her safely on board.

It was no surprise to blink the stinging water from her eyes to find that one set of those hands belonged to Joe. But she'd known that already, hadn't she? She had felt it…

It was only a skeleton staff that stayed on the Aratika Rescue Base for night shifts. By the time Maggie and Joe got back there, having transferred their patient to a road crew at the coastguard base, the crew on duty were out on a job and they knew the night manager would be manning the radio and probably catching up on paperwork in his office.

They needed to fill him in with any extra details he needed about their mission but there were more important things to do before they went upstairs from the locker room level. Despite the protective clothing that allowed them to get wet and work outside, delaying the development of hypothermia, at a certain point conditions could defeat the fabric technology.

'You're frozen,' Joe told Maggie. 'Look at how hard you're shivering. And you smell kind of like a dead fish.'

Maggie beamed at him. 'I know,' she

said, through chattering teeth. 'It was great, wasn't it?'

He had to smile back. 'It was a hot one, all right. And what we both need right now is a shower that's just as hot. You can go first.' He took the depleted pack of medical supplies to the far corner of the locker room. It would need to be sorted and restocked but that could wait until morning.

'J-Joe?'

Turning back, he could see Maggie's head poking out from the door that led to the showers and toilets.

'What's up?'

'Um…'

She sounded embarrassed, Joe decided. Or worried? He was closing the gap between them rapidly.

He saw what the problem was as soon as he stepped through the door to the shower room. Maggie was still shivering and her fingers were obviously too cold to be functioning as well as was needed to cope with all the Velcro fastenings and zips on her flight suit and boots.

She was colder than he'd realised. The need to look after her and treat the problem took over and Joe flipped the handle to get the shower running and warming up. Then he turned back to Maggie.

'Sit down,' he ordered. 'Let's get those boots off first.'

Maggie sat obediently on the bench seat facing the open shower. Joe's fingers felt clumsy but were co-operating well enough to unzip the boots and pull them off and then peel off her socks.

'Okay. Stand up again and we'll get this flight suit off. You should be able to manage the rest.'

He started undoing all the fastenings as soon as Maggie was on her feet again. This small room was getting warmer by the minute thanks to the steam from the running shower behind them. Joe realised he must have pushed the door shut without noticing when he'd come in to assist Maggie.

He peeled back the top of the flight suit and she grabbed onto his arm to keep her balance as she stepped out of the legs.

'All good?'

'Um…' Maggie held her hands out in front of her. They were still shaking. She tried to hook her fingers under the hem of the thermal top and then pull it up but she was laughing at the same time. 'I've gone a bit wobbly,' she said. 'I had no idea how cold I'd been getting.'

'Fine.' Joe was still in professional mode. This was no problem. He took hold of the hem of the long-sleeved shirt and pulled it up over Maggie's head.

Oh…*man*… His jaw dropped. How could she not have been wearing a bra under that shirt? The shock made it hard to raise his gaze from somewhere it should not be resting. Every instance of realising how attracted he was to Maggie coalesced in this moment into a desire like nothing he'd ever felt in his life. When he did manage to drag his gaze upwards, he saw something in Maggie's eyes that was even more of a shock.

Desire…

And it looked as fierce as what was threatening to produce the greatest test his self-control would ever have to deal with.

For a long, long moment, with the steam of the shower billowing gently around them, they held each other's gaze.

And then, before he'd started trying to analyse whatever was going on here, and without the slightest idea of who had made the first move, Joe was kissing Maggie.

Or Maggie was kissing him…

It didn't matter. It was rapidly becoming

the wildest, most exciting kiss he'd ever had in his life. The moment Maggie's tongue first touched his, inviting him to deepen that kiss, drove any rational thought behind a door in his brain that he had no immediate incentive to open.

Maggie wanted this. As much as he did.

How astonishing was that?

Oh…

If being in a steamy environment after getting too cold had made Maggie feel a bit wobbly, it was nothing to how weak this kiss was making her legs feel. She'd thought she'd known how good sex with Joe might be but she'd had *no* idea…

Maybe it was being enhanced by the adrenaline rush of the sea rescue job they'd both been challenged by. Or maybe her brain wasn't functioning perfectly thanks to the early stages of hypothermia. Whatever it was, this was an experience like nothing Maggie had ever had and she just knew that whatever alchemy had come together in this moment was never going to happen again.

This was a once-in-a-lifetime thing.

Normal rules could not be applied. This was a case of *carpe diem* if ever there was.

Seize the day. Or seize the moment, anyway…

Her fingers seemed to be working a whole lot better now. Enough to be getting past the fastenings of Joe's flight suit and trying to find some actual skin to touch. The tight fabric of her thermal leggings made it feel as though Joe's hands were inside them as he cupped her buttocks and pulled her closer. Close enough for her to realise that he was just as into this as she was.

Her groan of need against his lips seemed a signal to finish that blissful meeting of their mouths.

'*Maggie*…' Joe's voice was raw. 'We can't do this…'

She couldn't pull away. 'Why not? I… I want this, Joe…'

'Oh, *God*…so do I but…'

He pulled back far enough for Maggie to see his eyes. To see that desire had darkened them enough to appear black. How sexy was that?

'But it's not a good idea,' he ground out.

'Skin-to-skin contact is supposed to be a great way to treat hypothermia.'

Joe closed his eyes. He was clearly struggling. 'We work together, Maggie. We're *friends*…'

She had her hands on his back, beneath his thermal shirt. She could push her fingertips against his bare skin as she pressed herself closer. She didn't want to think about consequences right now. Whatever they were, they could deal with them later. This was a one-off. They would lose this moment very soon.

'Stop talking,' she whispered. 'Start kissing.'

His lips were on hers again almost instantly. Joe was just as carried away by whatever had ignited between them as Maggie was and that made this only more irresistible.

'Not safe...' she heard Joe groan against her lips.

Maggie managed to engage one small, rational part of her brain and extracted what she needed to know to give her a wash of relief. That was one normal rule that did need to be applied but it took only a heartbeat to be quite sure she was right. Her cycles were as regular as clockwork and she was close enough to the end to make any risk so small it was insignificant.

'It's safe,' she told Joe. 'I promise...'

CHAPTER FIVE

STUNNED.

That was the only word for it.

Joe had seen his own bewilderment reflected in Maggie's eyes in the immediate aftermath of that explosion of passion in the shower room of the Aratika Rescue Base.

He'd even articulated it, although admittedly it wasn't a particularly eloquent comment.

'What the hell was that?' he'd murmured as they were both trying to catch their breath.

Maggie had blinked back at him. She looked as if she was trying to smile but couldn't quite manage it. 'So… I guess your other hidden talent isn't knitting, after all?'

That had defused the sudden, alarmingly awkward tension between them as the reality of their nakedness and the intense lovemaking they had just shared sank in. Joe's breath had been expelled in a bark of laughter. Shaking his head, he'd dropped a quick kiss on Maggie's lips, gathered his discarded clothes and left her alone in the room that had been so steamy on far more than a literal level.

He was still bemused, if not shocked, by what had happened by the time he was dressed in a clean uniform and was nursing a cup of coffee in the upstairs staffroom. He had to wait for Maggie to appear. Not that he had any idea of what he was going to say to her but he couldn't just head home after that extraordinary encounter, could he?

It wasn't just the fact that what he'd considered for years as being a close friendship with no sexual agenda had just been proven so wrong in such an explosive manner. It was…the *sex*…

The most exciting—*satisfying*—sex he'd ever experienced in his life.

Was that due to the unexpectedness of it? he wondered. Or the risk that they could have been discovered by the crew returning to the base? Or perhaps it was the fact that it was the first time he'd ever had unprotected sex?

Oh…*help*… A bubble of panic rose in Joe's throat but he took a deep breath and swallowed it away. Maggie had assured him that it was safe and there was no one in the world he trusted more than Maggie.

But…what now?

They were colleagues. They had been friends for years. Neither of them had ever been attracted to each other before and they were the opposite of suitable candidates for anything more than a friendship because they wanted very different things from life. And Joe didn't want a relationship with Maggie because his relationships always fizzled out in the end and that was the last thing he wanted to happen with a friendship he valued so highly.

Maggie had made a joke about it so maybe it had been no big deal for her. Perhaps they could put it down to a moment of madness and pretend it had never happened. But that would mean it could never happen again. While Joe's head was telling him that was the sensible way forward here, his body was registering something like rebellion. How could you experience something like that and not want it to happen again—if nothing else, just to find out if it actually *had* been that good? A knot formed in his gut as he heard the clatter of boots on the stairs because he knew that just seeing Maggie again could be enough to reawaken the flames of the astonishing desire that had blindsided him.

Except it wasn't Maggie. Or it was, but she was following Cooper and his night shift partner, Jack, who were both carrying take-out containers of food. Maggie swerved without looking at Joe, heading to the kitchen counter to make herself a cup of coffee.

'Look at you,' Jack said to Joe. 'You look like you've been out windsurfing.' He sat down at the table. 'You should have paged us to let us know you were back on base. We could have picked you up some food.'

'How was the job?' Cooper pushed his chopsticks out of their paper packet. 'I'm dead jealous. I've been waiting for a coastguard callout since I started working here and there we were stuck in a multi-vehicle pile-up on the motorway.'

'It was awesome.' It was Maggie who answered Cooper. 'I think it might have been one of the most exciting callouts I've ever had.'

Joe swallowed hard. Was she referring to that wild boat ride? The experience of treating a patient in a very unusual location…?

Or could she be referring to what had happened when they'd arrived back on base?

Maybe Maggie would also be disappointed if they never got to do that again.

'How come you're still here?' Jack asked. 'We heard the ambulance being dispatched to meet the coastguards' boat ages ago.'

'We got pretty cold and wet,' Joe told them. 'Maggie had borderline hypothermia. We both needed a hot shower and a change of clothes.'

'Skin-to-skin contact might have been quicker,' Jack said around a mouthful of noodles.

Cooper laughed. 'And a lot more fun.'

Maggie sat down at the table with them. 'I'll remind you of that when you and Jack get sent out into the elements.'

'Hey…' Cooper was still grinning. 'I'm a happily married man.'

'And we're just good friends,' Jack added. 'Don't listen to those rumours.'

Maggie was laughing now, too. The atmosphere felt perfectly normal and that was the moment that Maggie finally caught Joe's gaze.

She looked happy, he realised. Sure, there was a question in her eyes but it was probably exactly the same question that was becoming a chant somewhere in the back of his own head.

Was it going to happen again?

'It can't happen again.'

Maggie needed to say it before Joe did. Because it might feel like less of a disappointment if it was her own decision?

But...*oh*...

She'd never had sex like that. Ever. She'd suspected that Joe might be good at it—he'd had plenty of practice over the years, after all—but she'd never expected that he could be *that* good.

The insanity had begun to recede rapidly in the wake of that extraordinary encounter, however. Even as Maggie had stood there in the steam, trying to catch her breath, she'd been increasingly aware of the enormity of what they'd just done and was reminding herself, in a flash of clarity, of all the reasons why she'd known she had to ignore the attraction she'd developed towards Joe.

It could destroy their friendship.

It could harm their working relationship.

In a moment of panic, Maggie had done the only thing she could think of that might lessen that enormity, and she'd cracked a joke about him demonstrating another one of his hidden talents. It wasn't enough, of course. She knew they needed to talk about it and that it had to happen fast and not be left to get more awkward to deal with, like that baby daddy conversation had become. But Cooper and Jack had arrived back on base as she'd headed upstairs and it seemed to take for ever until they got another callout and she was left in the staffroom alone with Joe.

He was staring at her now that she had opened what could be the most awkward conversation they'd ever had. She'd expected him to look relieved at her statement or possibly embarrassed at being reminded of what they'd done but it wasn't easy to interpret what she could see in those dark eyes. Wariness, she decided. He was waiting to see what she was going to say next. Whether it might be going to start with a 'but'.

'It shouldn't have happened in the first place.' She lowered her voice even more. 'And I think it was my fault.'

It was definitely her fault. Joe had tried to talk her out of it, hadn't he? She'd practically insisted. Told him to shut up and kiss her again.

'Sorry,' she added.

'Excuse me?' Joe's eyes had narrowed. 'Are you suggesting I've got no self-control?

If I'd wanted to stop, Maggie Lewis, I could have stopped. Okay?'

Maggie blinked. 'Okay…'

He'd wanted it? As much as she had? Well, well…

'I'm not saying it was a good idea,' Joe continued. 'But we're both adults. We both made that choice and we can both deal with it.'

Maggie nodded. 'But it can't happen again.'

'No.'

'We can still be friends, right?'

'Of course.'

'We can still go to the movies this weekend with Cooper and Fizz and Jack?'

'Sure.'

'And it won't be weird?'

'It might be a little bit weird,' Joe admitted. 'But we'll cope. And we're not going to talk about it again, okay? We're not even going to *think* about it at work.'

Maggie's nod emphasised her total agreement.

But then she caught Joe's gaze and a curious mix of apprehension and excitement tightened something deep inside her belly.

They both knew it was totally going to happen again.

* * *

'We did it again.' Joe pushed his hair back from his forehead as he let the rest of his breath out in a soft groan. 'When we said we wouldn't.'

'Yeah…but we had to find out, didn't we?'

'Find out what?'

'Whether it was going to be as good as the first time.'

'Yeah… I guess…'

'It was, wasn't it?'

'Oh, yeah… Possibly better…'

Joe was still wondering how that could actually be true. He was lying on his back, his eyes shut, still waiting for his heart rate to return to a normal level, still feeling the aftershocks of discovering that it wasn't some never-to-be-found-again alchemy of unusual elements that had made sex with Maggie so unbelievably awesome. It was simply the explosive combination of their personal chemistries.

This was a normal bed with no danger of being discovered, after a normal day off, although he couldn't currently remember the plot of the movie they'd gone to see with their friends. He'd been careful to use the usual level of protection he always used but none of that normality had diminished the excitement or satisfaction of that sex.

'Mmm…' Maggie sounded as if she was smiling. 'So what are we going to do now?'

'Don't know. It's still not a good idea, is it? We're friends. We work together.'

'It's not as though it's never happened before. Look at Cooper at Fizz.'

'That's completely different.'

'Why is it different?' He felt Maggie moving and turned his head to find she was propped up on one elbow.

'They got married.' Joe was aware of a beat of discomfort now. Was Maggie thinking that this new development in their relationship was leading somewhere? 'I don't want to marry you, Maggie.'

'Don't even go there,' Maggie agreed. 'I don't want to marry you, either. Believe me, I'll know who I want to marry— probably within a few minutes of meeting him. That's how it happened for my mum and dad. They took one look at each other and just *knew*. It certainly wasn't something I was thinking when I met you, mate.'

The relief was enough to make Joe smile into the darkness. 'You don't have to sound quite so adamant.'

'Hey… We both know we're on different

planets when it comes to a life partner. You told me your life story. I totally get that you don't want kids.'

'And you do.' Joe nodded.

'Six of them,' Maggie said.

Joe shuddered. *'Really?'*

'Yep.'

'Why?'

'I grew up as an only child. Don't get me wrong, I had a great childhood and I love my mum and dad to bits, but the best weekends or holidays I ever had were when I got to tag along with a friend's family and their brothers and sisters.' Maggie flopped back onto her pillow with a sigh. 'Good times. Like picnics or parties. Once, it was a combination. My friend Suzie had a huge family and I got invited to her picnic birthday party. There were balloons tied to the trees and fairy bread and games like…oh…do you remember Bullrush?'

'The game of tag where everybody who gets tagged turns into a chaser?'

'That's the one.'

'It got banned at my school for being dangerous. Too many kids got injured.'

'The fun police are everywhere,' Maggie muttered. 'We got to climb trees in those days, too. And jump off rocks and just have fun and...' a poignant note crept into her voice '...it was just so much more fun in a big family.'

'Fun's good,' Joe murmured. He wanted to change the subject, however. He could imagine a small Maggie in a scene like that, running around or jumping off rocks, her blonde curls bouncing and her face glowing with the joy of it all. He couldn't remember anything really joyous about his own childhood and he certainly didn't want a reminder of the less than happy memories. It was in the past and best left there. Besides, that wasn't actually what they'd been talking about.

'So we're on the same page, then. This isn't something that's going anywhere?'

'No.'

It was Joe's turn to prop himself up on his elbow. 'No, we're not on the same page?'

Maggie grinned up at him. 'No, it's not going anywhere. We're both adults, Joe. We're both single. We're not doing anything wrong.'

'It could mess with our friendship.'

'Not if we're both on the same page and we're not expecting it to go anywhere. Maybe it shouldn't have started, but it did and you didn't exactly have to twist my arm to come home with you after the movie to-night, did you?'

'No.' In fact, whose idea had it been to keep the evening going after Cooper had declared that he and Fizz needed to head home straight after the movie because his pregnant wife needed her rest? Joe couldn't remember. Much like their encounter in the shower room at the base, it had been a mutual and pretty much simultaneous choice.

'And maybe it's not going to last long at all but while it's fun, is there anything wrong with enjoying it? Having some fun?' The tip of Maggie's tongue appeared as she ran it across her bottom lip. 'I don't know about you, but it's a very long time since I've had quite *this* much fun.'

'Mmm…' Joe's head had begun dipping the moment he'd seen that tip of her tongue. Any fears of ruining their friendship or working relationship were evaporating in the face of what Maggie seemed to be offering, which was a 'no strings, no expectations' enjoyment of the best sex ever. What man in his right mind was going to argue with that?

His lips were on Maggie's by the time she finished speaking so he only just managed a couple of extra words. 'Fun's good…'

* * *

Oh…thank *goodness*…

Maggie stayed where she was for a long minute, sitting on the toilet with her head in her hands as she breathed the longest sigh of relief ever.

The last few days hadn't been fun at all.

She'd been late with her period. She had been so absolutely sure that she had been in the safest possible part of her cycle that night in the shower room but then her period hadn't arrived and it was *always* on time. She'd actually been on the verge of a trip to the pharmacy to buy a pregnancy test kit. Well, to be honest, she should have done it days ago but she'd managed to maintain a state of almost complete denial.

She didn't need to go down that route now and the wave of relief was overpowering. She even had an explanation for the unexpected blip in her regularity because that was often due to stress, wasn't it? And Maggie *had* been stressed about that falling out with Joe. Not as stressed as she'd been the last few days, mind you.

Maggie wasn't even going to try and imagine what it might have been like having to explain to Joe that she'd got her timing wrong enough for the consequences of that first time together to be disastrous. And an accidental pregnancy would have been a disaster, she had no doubts about that. Any thoughts of planned single parenthood had been banished for the moment in the wake of that conversation with Laura, but if she ever contemplated it again it would definitely be some anonymous sample from a bank. Involving anyone she knew would make things impossibly complicated.

Involving Joe would be the end of the world...

Her relief must have shown in her smile when she came out of the bathroom and ran to join Joe as he was getting into the chopper in response to their pager signalling a callout.

'You look like you've won the lottery,' Joe said.

'It's been too quiet today, that's all. I was getting bored.'

'This should do the trick then. If a local crew has called for urgent backup it could be a critical case.'

Maggie nodded as she clipped her harness together. With the kind of injuries that could be caused by being trampled by animals that weighed half a ton, this could be a challenging job.

Just the kind they both loved.

A 'hot' one.

It took only a few minutes' flying time to reach the farm on the hills behind one of the outer city suburbs.

'There's a mob of sheep down there.'

'We'll buzz them and come around again. That should persuade them to give us some room.' Andy the pilot and crewman Nick were both peering down at the intended landing site for the rescue helicopter.

'The horses might be more of a worry.' Maggie was also focussed on the ground below as sheep began to scatter to get away from the noisy machine overhead.

'You don't like horses?' Joe sounded surprised. 'Think of them as motorbikes with brains and you'll get on just fine.'

'Motorbikes don't club together and run you over. Where's the bunch of horses that trampled our patient?'

'They've been shifted to the next paddock,' Andy said. 'But there hasn't been time to round up the sheep. It's okay…looks like we've got plenty of room now. Let's have another go…'

The helicopter tilted as it turned and Maggie could see the horses now, well away from the cluster of people, some farm vehicles and an ambulance.

Joe had the doors open by the time the skids touched the grass. Maggie shoved her arms through the straps of the pack and they both crouched, exchanging a glance as they ran under the still turning rotors of the helicopter.

There was more than just the adrenaline rush of facing an unknown challenge together that was shared in that glance, though. On Maggie's part it had a lot to do with the relief she was feeling but she knew the message that Joe was conveying in that split second of eye contact and she could agree with it wholeheartedly—an acknowledgement that what was going on in their personal lives at the moment was not interfering in any way with their working relationship. If anything, it was making it better.

They'd been a tight team already but something had definitely changed since they'd become so much closer out of work hours. They both knew their 'fling', or whatever it was, couldn't continue long term and the relief Maggie had felt with the arrival of her period today was an indication that it probably needed to end sooner rather than later because there was more at stake here than simply a physical relationship but…not just yet…

This new layer to her working relationship with Joe was amazing—a side effect of the recent change to their friendship? Was it the intimate knowledge of each other that had added a new depth to that friendship? Or was it that their friendship had made sex such a different experience, adding humour and tenderness into the mix?

Whatever it was, it was special but even the flash of a glance that had reminded her of the bond between them couldn't interfere with the professional focus Maggie knew they both had right now. If anything, for her, it made that focus sharper. She was working with the person she trusted more than anyone on the planet. Her best friend who was, temporarily, also her lover. She wanted to do the best job she possibly could, not only for her patient but so that Joe would be as proud to have her as his partner as she was to have him.

A man with a small girl in his arms and a taller boy pressed against his leg were standing beside the figure on the ground as Maggie and Joe ran towards them, their packs on their backs. His face, creased with worry, relaxed a little as they arrived.

'Thanks for coming, guys.'

'No worries,' Joe said.

'This is Caroline,' one of the ambulance officers introduced them, and then started his handover. 'She's thirty-six. Came out this afternoon to check on one of the horses and got trampled.'

'It wasn't their fault.' Caroline was conscious. She looked pale and as if she was in pain but being fully alert was a reassuring sign that her head injury was not too severe. 'I was trying to put a halter on Star and I accidently touched the electric fence behind me. She got a shock and bolted and that panicked all the others. I got knocked down and trodden on a few times.'

'She's got a head injury,' the ground crew paramedic said. 'Pupils are uneven. She's also complaining of sore ribs and an injury to her lower leg. No breathing problems so far and vital signs all good. She wasn't knocked out and GCS was fifteen when we arrived. She used her mobile phone to call her husband for help.'

'That's me,' the man with the children said. 'I'm Barry.'

'What's wrong with Mummy?' The little girl in his arms looked even more terri-fied than her older brother. 'Why can't she get up?'

'She's got sore bits, sweetheart.' It was Maggie who looked up to smile reassur-ingly at the child. 'That's why we need to look after her. Like Mummy looks after you when you've got sore bits.'

The child nodded. 'I felled over yesterday. Mummy put a plaster on my knee, see?'

'I do. It's a big plaster.'

'It was sore. But I didn't cry.'

'That was very brave.'

'I'm being brave, too, Lucy.' Caroline turned her head to smile up at her daughter. 'Just like you.'

'Were you lying on your back or your front when you fell?' Joe asked. He shone a small torch into each of her eyes. Uneven pupils could be a variant of normal so the way they reacted to light might be more of an indica-tion of how serious the head injury could be. Both pupils were reactive to the light, which was another reassuring finding.

'My front.' Caroline closed her eyes and groaned as Joe began to check the swollen area of her scalp.

'She's had two point five milligrams of morphine.'

'What's your pain score now, Caroline? Out of ten, with zero being no pain and ten the worst you can think of?'

'About six…a bit better than it was before.'

'Where does it hurt the most?'

'My leg…and my head.'

'Maggie will top up that pain relief a bit for you. I'm just going to check your ear.' He turned to look in his pack for the otoscope, only to find Maggie was holding it out to him. 'Thanks, mate.'

She was already busy on her next task as he crouched low to shine the light of the otoscope into Caroline's ear and he knew that as soon as she'd given Caroline some more morphine Maggie would be assessing the leg that was causing so much pain.

Sure enough, as he registered the concerning patch of colour on his patient's eardrum that could indicate a collection of blood beneath, he could hear Maggie's calm voice.

'Push your foot against my hand… Okay, now pull up against it… Where does that hurt?'

They were both delving into their packs for supplies a minute or two later. Joe needed a bandage to hold a dressing in place on Caroline's scalp and Maggie was finding a splint for her lower leg.

'Haemotympanun,' Joe told Maggie quietly. 'But her neurological status seems stable.'

'I can't be sure if it's a fracture or muscle injury to her leg but it's swollen and painful enough to make me query compartment syndrome. Limb baselines are lower than they were when the first crew arrived.'

'We'd better get this show on the road, then.' Joe reached for his radio. 'Nick? Could you bring the stretcher, please?'

Maggie splinted Caroline's leg. As the ambulance crew helped Joe lift their patient and then secure her to the helicopter's stretcher, she turned to talk to Caroline's husband.

'We're going to take Caroline in to the emergency department of the Royal. She's going to need a scan to rule out a possible skull fracture and an orthopaedic specialist to deal with the leg injury.'

Lucy burst into tears. 'No...don't take my Mummy away.'

'It's okay, Luce,' Barry said. 'We'll go in the car. You'll see Mummy again very soon.'

'You will,' Maggie said. 'But would you like to give her a big kiss first? And tell her how brave she is?'

From the corner of his eye, as Joe did up one of the strap buckles that would keep Caroline secure on the stretcher if they hit any turbulence, he could see Maggie hold out her arms and the little girl respond by reaching back. Maggie settled the child on one hip and then held out her hand again to the silent, scared-looking boy.

'I'll bet Mummy needs a kiss from you, too.'

'I do…' Caroline's voice wobbled but she managed to hold it together while she exchanged kisses and reassured her children. Then it was Barry's turn to lean over the stretcher and kiss his wife.

'We'll be there as soon as. Love you…'

Caroline just nodded, clearly unable to trust her voice as Joe and Nick began to carry her towards the helicopter. Joe looked back to see Maggie giving Lucy a cuddle before transferring her back into her father's arms. For just a moment he saw her as part of that family picture of a man and woman and two gorgeous kids.

Add in a few more kids and it was exactly what she wanted in her own life.

Exactly what he might have wanted in his life, if things had been different. And Maggie would have been the woman he might well have chosen to be the mother of those children.

But that was never going to happen and if he was a true friend he'd be encouraging her to get out there and find the partner— hopefully the love of her life—who would be able to give her what she wanted so much. He shouldn't be wasting her time by keeping her distracted with a relationship that was no more than a 'friends with benefits' one that really shouldn't have started in the first place.

He was still watching as Maggie began to run towards him to catch up. The sound of the rotors got louder as Andy readied the aircraft for take-off.

She looked different for some reason, he thought, turning back to direct the loading of the stretcher into the helicopter. Some kind of glow about her despite the lines of concern on her face that he knew were all about their patient and her family. Or was it just because he'd started to see her as so much more than simply his friend or colleague? Like the way he'd noticed different things about Maggie when he'd realised how attractive she was.

Maggie Lewis was just a stunning human being, that's what it was. And if he could have given her what she wanted, Joe would have been at the head of the queue. He knew perfectly well how easy it would be to fall in love with Maggie if he stepped past that roadblock. But he also knew that that wasn't going to happen, which meant he would never be in any queue of potential life partners.

It wasn't fair to hold Maggie back. They needed to stop what was happening between them before it went on too long.

Before it got too difficult to stop because it was so damn good?

Maggie pulled the door shut behind her, gave him a thumbs-up sign and settled herself in the seat at the head of Caroline's stretcher where she could both monitor her patient's condition and supply any needed reassurance.

Joe buckled himself into the seat at the side of the stretcher where he was in a good position to reach any equipment and provide any treatment needed on the short flight to the hospital.

He spared only the briefest of another thought concerning Maggie.

Yes, it had to stop.

But hopefully not just yet…

CHAPTER SIX

'WE'RE JUST GOOD FRIENDS.' But Joe's sideways glance at Maggie held a question. *Have you been talking to someone about us?*

Her subtle headshake served as both a reassuring response to Joe and a sign of impatience with Adam, the Aratika HEMS doctor on duty with Cooper today, who'd asked if there was something going on between Joe and Maggie.

'Looked like more than that when I saw you both out dancing in that bar last week,' he persisted.

Maggie shrugged. 'We're both single. We felt like a night out. It's no big deal.'

It wasn't a big deal. Yes, she and Joe saw each other once or twice a week and sometimes went out and always enjoyed great sex and, yes, it should have stopped by now after nearly two months but it was still fun and neither of them had anyone else waiting in the wings, so why not?

'Oh…beware…' Fizz turned from where she was reading notices on the board in the staffroom. 'That's how it started with me and Cooper. We were just good friends and look at me now…' She patted her protruding belly.

'How long now, Fizz?' Joe sounded like he was keen to change the subject.

'Three months. And I was three months along when I got married, which means… Hey, Coop. It's our three-month anniversary today. Where are you taking me to celebrate?'

'That's why I've snuck you on base for one of Shirley's Sunday roasts. Best meal in town.'

'Aww…' Shirley was stirring a large pot on the stovetop. 'You're a good boy, Cooper Sinclair. I knew you were going to be from the moment you arrived here. I'll be ready for you to carve this meat soon. I'm just finishing the gravy.'

'Can I help?' Maggie joined Shirley at the bench.

'You could drain those carrots and then put some butter and parsley on them.'

'It's no wonder I'm putting on weight, Shirley. Between your roast dinners and all

those cakes and cookies, I've got no hope.'
She might have to make a bit of an effort,
in fact. Her uniform trousers had been noticeably tight when she'd put them on this
morning.

'You just need to do a bit more dancing,
then.' Shirley's glance implied that she knew
exactly what was going on between Maggie
and Joe and wasn't about to have any wool
pulled over her eyes.

Maggie made a mumbled sound of agreement. She threw a knob of butter and the already chopped parsley on top of the carrots
and put the lid of the pot back on.

'I'll put the plates in the warming drawer,
shall I?'

'They're already in there.'

Shirley was a stickler for doing things the
right way and that included warmed plates
for her food. And despite the unspoken rule
that places at the table for Sunday lunch were
only for the crews on duty that day, nobody
was going to complain about Cooper's wife
being included. Fizz had had to give up her
shifts on base while she was pregnant and
everybody missed her company, especially
Maggie.

She leaned her head against her friend's

shoulder for a moment as Fizz came up and slung her arm over Maggie's shoulders.

'Glad you came,' she murmured. 'I don't get to see you that often these days.'

'You should come and visit, then. Instead of going out dancing with Joe.' Fizz's tone was teasing. She didn't think there was anything going on between them and why would she? Everybody knew that Maggie and Joe had worked together for years with nothing happening. What had changed to make Adam suspicious, not to mention Shirley being convinced? Was the new bond that had made them a closer team than ever somehow visible from the outside?

Fizz was sniffing appreciatively. 'I'm starving. That gravy smells divine, Shirley.'

'Secret ingredient.' Shirley nodded. 'And you should be starving. You're eating for two.'

'That doesn't excuse my current gluttony.' Fizz grinned. 'So what's the secret ingredient, then?'

'If I told you that, it wouldn't be a secret any more, now, would it?'

Maggie laughed along with Fizz but she took a deeper sniff, wondering if she could work out what the mysterious ingredient could be. Oddly, none of the aromas from the food smelled as nice as they usually did. There was a note in the mix that made her feel slightly queasy, in fact.

Fizz had her head much closer to the pot as she sniffed. 'Aha...could it be garlic?'

Shirley's chin came up. 'Not telling. Cooper? You want to come and carve this meat?' She opened the oven door with one hand, picking up her oven gloves with the other. 'Adam, why don't you make yourself useful and come and get these veggies out of the oven and onto the table? I'm too old to be lifting that heavy tray.'

The laughter was more general this time. Shirley might be in her seventies but she was ageless. A much-loved institution now and nobody wanted to think about her not being an honorary member of the staff. She'd been a part of Aratika for longer than Maggie had been, having started to supply the crews with her wonderful baking after her son's life had been saved by a helicopter crew many years ago. She'd started coming in to cook breakfast just after Maggie had been lucky enough to join the team five years ago and the Sunday lunch tradition had begun not long after that.

Adam pushed his chair back and came towards the kitchen area but Shirley was already pulling a tray from the oven—the muffin tin that had a dozen of her famous Yorkshire puddings in it. The heavier oven tray with the delicious array of roasted potatoes and other vegetables was on a lower rack.

'I'll need those oven gloves,' Adam said.

Shirley straightened, holding the muffin tin in her hands. Cooper was off to one side, sharpening the carving knife, and Maggie and Fizz were still standing by the sink when it happened. The muffin tray slid from Shirley's hand to crash on the floor, sending the Yorkshire puddings flying in all directions. At almost the same instant, Shirley crumpled, clutching at her chest. Adam caught her.

'Here…sit down, Shirley.'

Maggie was crouched in front of the older woman by the time Adam had lowered her to sit on the floor with her back against one of the kitchen cabinets.

'What's happening, Shirley? Have you got chest pain?'

Shirley nodded. 'Right here…' Her fist was pressed against the centre of her chest. 'Oh…it feels like I've got an elephant sitting on top of me. It's hard to breathe…'

'I'll grab a life pack…' Joe ran from the staffroom, Cooper on his heels.

'Do you have any medical conditions we should know about?' Fizz had her hand on Shirley's wrist. 'High blood pressure? Angina?'

Shirley nodded. 'I take pills for my blood pressure. I don't have angina. That's what my Stan had, before he died with his heart attack.' She had gone very pale now and Maggie could see beads of sweat on her forehead. 'Is that what this is? Am I having a heart attack?'

'That's what we're going to find out.'

Joe and Cooper were back with a life pack, a medical pack and an oxygen cylinder. They took cushions from one of the couches in the staffroom and made Shirley more comfortable, propping her up with an oxygen mask in place as they all tried to contribute to finding out what was happening and treating it by getting vital signs, including a twelve-lead ECG and putting an IV line in so they could give her some pain relief.

Don, the base manager, came into the room, closely followed by Andy. 'Can we do anything to help?' he asked.

'Maybe get a stretcher from the back of an

ambulance. We'll be heading for the Royal pretty soon.'

'Chew this up for me, Shirley.' Fizz lifted the oxygen mask, ready to give Shirley the white tablet.

'What is it?'

'An aspirin. I'll get you a sip of water to wash it down.' Maggie found Joe and Cooper both still studying the ECG graph.

'It's not huge but there's definitely widespread ST segment elevation. And some T wave changes starting.'

'We need to get her into ED as quickly as possible,' Joe nodded. 'And up to the catheter laboratory if needed.'

'You and Maggie take one of the ambulances,' Don said. 'Adam and Cooper can cover any helicopter callout for the moment. I'll call in some extra staff so you can stay with Shirley for a while.'

'I'm going, too,' Fizz said. 'I can stay as long as it takes.'

'But…' Shirley pulled down her mask so that they could hear her clearly. 'But you'll all miss your Sunday lunch…'

'We're thinking about all the Sunday lunches to come,' Fizz teased her gently. 'It's far more important to us to make sure you're going to be around for a long time yet.'

Joe drove the ambulance to the Royal and Maggie and Fizz stayed in the back, looking after Shirley and giving her the best reassurance that they could, knowing that it could contribute to keeping her safe from a potential cardiac arrest.

'Just relax,' Maggie told her. 'Keep your breathing nice and slow.'

'You're going to be well looked after,' Fizz added. 'They'll want to do another ECG in Emergency and they'll take some blood tests. It's quite likely that they'll take you up to the catheter laboratory after that.'

'Why?'

'Because that's where they can see exactly what's going on in the arteries in your heart and, if any of them are blocked, they can fix it. You'll come out as good as new. Better, even.'

Maggie could see the fear in Shirley's eyes so she squeezed her hand. 'Don't worry... we're not going to leave you by yourself.'

They stayed with Shirley for her initial tests and then waited for the results of the blood tests, which came back swiftly, and then waited again until the catheter laboratory staff on call for a Sunday could get back to the Royal and set up for angiography. They accompanied Shirley in the lift and Maggie even offered to put on a lead apron and stay with her in the laboratory but Shirley refused.

'I'm fine… Whatever they gave me to relax is working very well. I'd much rather you all went and found yourselves something to eat. You said you were starving, Fizz, and that was a long time ago now. You go and look after yourself and that bubba. Maggie and Joe can make sure that you do.'

So they went back to the staffroom in the emergency department to wait until Shirley's procedure was finished and they could see her settled into the coronary care unit. They bought packets of sandwiches from a vending machine and Fizz busied herself making hot drinks for them all.

Maggie took a sip of hers. 'Oh…' She screwed up her nose. 'This coffee tastes really weird. Disgusting, even. Is it really stale or something?'

Joe tried his. 'Tastes perfectly okay to me,' he said. 'Nothing wrong with it.'

Fizz laughed. 'Maybe you're pregnant, Mags. Coffee was the first thing I went off. I can only drink tea now.'

It was a mistake to catch Joe's gaze but Maggie hadn't been able to stop it happening. She could see the way his eyes darkened, as if his pupils had dilated due to shock. She tried to send him a reassuring message. It wasn't true. It couldn't be. They'd been very careful ever since that first time and she'd had a period after that.

When was that, exactly? Maggie counted back in her head as she dragged her gaze away from Joe's. She started peeling the plastic cover off her pack of sandwiches. It was over a month ago so she must be due for her next period anytime. It was okay. She'd had a fright last time and it had been okay.

Fizz had been watching the interaction between them. 'Oh, my goodness,' she murmured into the silence that had fallen. 'So Adam was right?'

'It's not a thing,' Maggie said. 'We really are just good friends. And I'm *not* pregnant.'

She could feel Joe's gaze on her as she picked up her sandwich and took a bite. She could actually feel what he was thinking— that it really was time they stopped sleeping together when even the thought of something going wrong was a threat to their friendship and working relationship.

The mixture of bread, cheese and ham in her mouth suddenly felt like cardboard and it became a mission to swallow it.

'You don't like your sandwich?' Fizz asked. 'Want to swap with one of mine?'

Maggie shook her head. 'I might be coming down with something,' she muttered. 'I'll get a glass of water.'

She stood up but then sat down again, holding her head in her hands.

'What's going on?' Joe demanded.

'Felt a bit dizzy, that's all.'

'Could be low blood sugar,' Fizz said. 'Did you eat breakfast this morning?'

'No...but I don't usually eat breakfast, anyway.'

Joe had his fingers on her wrist. 'Could be low blood pressure. Her radial pulse is quite weak. And a bit rapid.'

'Come with me.' Fizz stood up and waited for Maggie to get up again. 'I'm going to check you out.'

'Good idea,' Joe said. 'Need a hand?'

'No. Finish your lunch.' Fizz glanced at her abandoned meal. 'We'll be back soon.'

She took Maggie into an empty cubicle. 'Get up on the bed,' she instructed. 'And tell me what's really going on.'

'I told you. I'm probably coming down with some bug.'

Fizz was wrapping the blood-pressure cuff around her arm. 'Symptoms?'

'Nothing much. I just feel a bit off and my skin feels odd. Like my clothes are uncomfortable.' Maggie used her free hand to undo the button on her trousers. 'That's better...' She lay back on the pillow and closed her eyes.

Fizz was silent as she slowly let the air out of the cuff and took her blood-pressure reading. 'Your BP's fine,' she told Maggie.

In the silence that followed, Maggie wondered if Fizz was finding the kit to test her blood sugar but then she opened her eyes to find that her friend hadn't actually moved from the side of the bed. And that she was staring at where she'd opened the button of her trousers. At the red marks her waistband had left on her skin. Her friend's voice was quiet when she spoke.

'You're quite sure you're not pregnant?'

Maggie swallowed hard. She still hadn't finished adding up the weeks in her head. 'I might be a little late,' she confessed. 'But I was late last month, too, and that was okay. I think it was just due to stress.'

'Normal period last time?'

'A bit light, I guess. Normal enough.'

'Are your breasts tender?'

'They always are a bit when I'm about to get my period.' Maggie pushed herself up.

'I *can't* be pregnant, Fizz. There was only one time when we weren't super-careful and that was ages ago and, as I said, I've had a period since then.'

'A late one. You do realise how common it is to have some bleeding in early pregnancy, don't you? Like, twenty five percent of women.'

'Don't say that,' Maggie muttered. Of course she realised. She'd been a midwife. Had the rush of relief of believing she wasn't pregnant conveniently washed away that particular bit of knowledge?

Fizz put her hand on Maggie's abdomen. 'Can I have a feel?'

'Sure.' Maggie lay down again just to buy herself some thinking time. Even if the unthinkable had happened and she was pregnant, surely Fizz wouldn't be able to feel anything.

'Hmm…'

'What?'

'I'm absolutely sure I can feel your uterus and that's not easy to do unless someone is getting close to twelve weeks along. That would fit with your weight gain as well. And thinking that your coffee tasted strange.'

Maggie shook her head. 'Nope. Can't be.'

Except that she was counting weeks in her

head again. Back to the night of that coast-guard job. If she *had* become pregnant then she would be...about ten or eleven weeks along now.

Oh... *God*...

'Is it Joe's?' Fizz asked quietly.

It was hard to speak through a suddenly dry mouth. 'Don't say anything,' she whispered.

'Of course not. Are you going to tell him?'

She didn't have a choice, did she? 'I need to figure out how to do that first,' she said. 'It'll be the last thing he wants to hear.'

'You're not looking too thrilled yourself.'

That was such an understatement that Maggie let out a huff of laughter. And then she found herself blinking back tears. 'What am I going to do, Fizz?'

'Get some irrefutable evidence, for starters. I'd eat my hat if I was wrong but stranger things have happened. You could pee in a cup and I'll test it for you here, if you like. Or take a blood test.'

Maggie shook her head. 'No. What if Joe comes in?' She was doing up the button on her trousers again. 'I'll do it tomorrow.'

She knew what the result would be. It all made perfect sense now. She'd just been looking the other way, even when she'd had reason to suspect it right from the start when her period was unusually late. But, no, she'd stuck her head in the sand and pretended everything was fine because she'd decided that it had to be that way. She'd glanced at the potential consequences and put them in the 'too hard' basket—and grabbed at what seemed to be a reprieve with both hands.

'You'll need to get a proper obstetric check-up as soon as possible. And an ultrasound. That'll give you a more accurate estimate of dates. Hey…' Fizz put her arms around Maggie. 'It'll be okay, hon.'

Reassurance might be a good thing when someone was having a heart attack, to keep the heart rate down and oxygen level up, but it didn't feel at all useful at the moment. Or believable.

It wasn't going to be okay.

Not at all.

'You should go home.'

'I'm fine. Fizz told you there was nothing wrong with me.'

'You've been weird all afternoon.'

Joe opened the fridge in the staffroom and looked at all the food that had been packed up and stored. It looked like nobody had had any appetite for Shirley's roast dinner after it had been interrupted in such a dramatic fashion. Cooper and Adam were out on what would be their last job for their shift and the night duty staff were due to arrive soon. Don was upstairs in his office and Maggie was sitting on one of the couches, her legs tucked up, staring into space, which was so unlike her it was disturbing. She never sat and did nothing like that. She talked to people or read something or busied herself in some way and she did it with an enthusiasm that made those around her think she was making the most of every minute of her life. It was one of the things Joe had always loved about Maggie—how good you felt in her company—how much brighter your day became.

He walked over to her now and perched on the arm at the other end of the sofa.

'Shirley's going to be fine, you know. She sailed through that angioplasty. She'll be home in a couple of days and probably here cooking breakfast by the end the of the week. Or another Sunday roast.'

Everybody loved Shirley's Sunday roasts but, for Joe, they were even more special because they felt like the kind of family ritual he'd never had as a child. Shirley was almost more of a mother to him than his own mother had ever been.

'I know that.' But Maggie's smile looked a little forced.

'So what's the matter?'

Maggie gaze slid away from his. Had he said something to upset her? Joe thought back to when things had started to get weird this afternoon. Maybe Maggie was coming down with something and it was just too early for Fizz to have picked it up when she'd had a look.

Or maybe it wasn't something *he'd* said.

'It was that coffee thing, wasn't it? That's when things got weird. When Fizz suggested you might be pregnant.'

Maggie still wasn't looking at him. In fact, she looked as if she was frozen now. Not even breathing. A shiver started at the back of Joe's neck and trickled all the way down his spine.

'You are…aren't you?'

Finally, slowly, Maggie turned her head and looked up to meet his gaze and the truth was blindingly obvious.

Joe swallowed hard. 'I don't understand. We've been so careful.'

'Except that first time.'

'*What?* How far along *are* you?'

'I'm not sure exactly. Fizz thinks it's close to twelve weeks. If it was that first night that would mean about eleven weeks.'

Joe closed his eyes, grappling with emotions that were rushing at him like tsunamis. Panic? Anger? He managed to keep his tone level.

'And how long have you known?'

'I still haven't done a test. It didn't even occur to me until Fizz was so sure but it makes sense. She reminded me that twenty five percent of women can have bleeding in early pregnancy that they might think is a normal period...' Her voice trailed away. 'When it isn't.'

Joe could hear the ice around his words. 'You told me it was safe. You *promised* me that it was safe.'

'I thought it was. I truly believed it was.'

'Really?' Joe was losing the battle to keep those overwhelming emotions at bay. He got to his feet, hoping that a bit of pacing might help. It didn't. He swung back to face her.

'I'm not sure I believe you, Maggie. It's a bit of a coincidence, isn't it? You tell me how desperate you are to have a baby and then...' His brain was taking him back to that steamy night. He could hear echoes of words.

His words—*We can't do this*...

Maggie's words—*Why not? I want this, Joe*...

But what had she wanted so much? Sex with him or the possibility of becoming pregnant? Panic about what the future might hold could wait. Right now, this was about being betrayed. By the one person he would never have believed could do that.

'I *trusted* you...' His voice was loud now. He never shouted at anybody, ever, but this was getting alarmingly close.

Maggie was scrambling to her feet as well. 'I know. I'm sorry, Joe. This is as much of a shock to me as it is to you.'

'I don't think so. You *wanted* this. You were *planning* to be a single mother.'

'No...' Maggie's voice was raised now. 'I mean, I *thought* I wanted it but then I changed my mind. And even if I hadn't changed my mind, I wouldn't have wanted it to be like *this*.'

'What the hell is going on in here?'

They both turned to find Don Smith, Aratika's manager, at the foot of the staircase that led to the upstairs management office and control desk.

'We can all hear you yelling at each other.'

'It's private,' Joe snapped.

'Not any more.' Don was walking towards

them, shaking his head. 'Are you pregnant, Maggie?'

'I think so...' Joe saw the moment the tears welled up in her eyes and one escaped to roll down her cheek. 'Yes... I'm sure I am. I haven't done an official test but it all adds up.'

He didn't like to see Maggie cry but there was nothing about any of this that Joe was liking. Quite the opposite. This might, in fact, qualify as being one of the worst days of his life.

Don glanced at Joe. 'You're the father, I take it?'

'Apparently.' It was a cruel thing to say. Maggie would never cheat on anybody, even if it hadn't been a 'real' relationship.

Don was looking at Maggie now. 'And you're keeping the baby?'

He heard Maggie gasp. He was shocked himself that Don would even ask.

'You might think it's none of my business,' Don said, 'but it actually is. I want you to take a few days' leave, Maggie. You've got a lot to think about.'

'But—'

'You'll have to step down from active duty. We'll find you another position. If nothing else, I don't think you and Joe can work together again. Judging by the last ten minutes, patient care could be compromised by the issues between you two.' He held his hand up as Maggie opened her mouth to say something else. 'I don't want to know about your private lives but I'm not having it affect the operation of this rescue base.' He glanced at his watch. 'It's nearly changeover. Go home, both of you.' He was shaking his head as he headed back towards the stairs. 'I think we've all had enough of today.'

'He can't do that,' Maggie whispered. 'He practically just fired me…'

'He can. And he did.' Joe had never been this angry in his life. He walked away from Maggie before he found himself saying something he might later regret and he didn't stop moving until he'd left the building and wrenched his car door open.

'Hey, Joe!' One of the night shift crew was getting out of her car. 'You getting off early for good behaviour?'

'Something like that.' Joe actually managed to find a smile. 'Have a good one, Angie.'

He dropped into his driver's seat and slammed the door shut, backing out and taking off and deliberately ignoring what he could see in his peripheral vision.

Maggie, standing by her bike, her helmet in her hands, but she wasn't moving to put it on. She was watching him leave.

He didn't want to speak to her again right now. He didn't even want to look at her. He was having his life ripped apart and there was nothing at all he could do about it. He was being forced into becoming a father when it was the last thing he'd ever wanted to be. He was losing the colleague who'd always been his favourite person to work with. And he was losing someone he'd thought would be one of his best friends for life.

This was worse than betrayal.

Right now it felt like complete destruction.

There was only one place he could be that might help him deal with emotions that were trying to make his head explode. Instead of making the turn that would have taken him home to his apartment, Joe turned the other way. Towards a beach that he knew would provide a challenge. It was a good thing he kept his board and sail strapped to his roof rack most of the time. He must have known that, one day, it might feel like he needed the wind and the waves in order to stay sane.

It felt like it might actually save his life today.

CHAPTER SEVEN

SHE'D KNOWN IT could be the end of her world as she knew it.

But she hadn't realised it would feel quite *this* devastating.

On more than one occasion of being slowed down or stuck in city traffic as Maggie made her way home, she had to swipe at the tears streaking her cheeks beneath her visor.

This was her fault.

How *stupid* had she been?

Classic signs of pregnancy and she'd simply ignored them all. The tender breasts and weight gain. Today hadn't been the first time she'd thought food tasted or smell wrong, either. She'd even dismissed feeling nauseated last week as being due to a greasy takeaway the night before.

Blind. And stupid.

No wonder Joe thought she'd done this

on purpose. Who wouldn't after hearing her banging on about being happy to become a single mother?

And no wonder he hated her right now. He was probably relieved that she wasn't going to be allowed to be on the front line of any emergency service while she was pregnant and, as from tomorrow, he would have a new partner as part of his crew.

Oh...help... Maggie swiped her face again and gave an enormous sniff. She'd betrayed her best friend and nobody was going to believe it was the last thing she would have done intentionally. She'd lost the job she loved so much as well. She'd probably have to go and help Danny with uniforms and supplies and restocking the kits. Or she'd be assigned to a research project and be stuck behind a desk collecting data and putting it into spreadsheets.

Fizz had had to give up being on the helicopters due to her pregnancy, too, but at least she was able to keep working in the emergency department for as long as she wanted. She also had the support of a loving partner who'd probably been thrilled when they'd discovered they had a baby on the way.

This was Joe's worst nightmare, wasn't it?

As Maggie turned up the road that led up

the valley to her house, she was still thinking about Fizz. Or rather about her wedding night. About when Joe had opened up and told her why he would never want to bring a child into the world.

Kids get caught in the flak... They can grow up thinking that it's their fault. That, no matter how hard they try, they can never fix things...

Maggie could remember very clearly how much she'd wanted to cuddle that small, unhappy boy hidden beneath the surface of Joe's adult life.

The urge to put her arms around him and hold him now was even more powerful.

Because she cared. So much. She loved him.

Not just as her best friend and favourite workmate.

How broken she was feeling right now told Maggie that perhaps she didn't just love Joe in terms of friendship. Was she *in* love with him? Was that why the thought of not having him in her life from now on was ripping her apart so painfully?

Something else she'd been conveniently blind about, maybe. Had she really believed that they could just 'have fun' together and then go back to their old friendship with nothing fundamentally changed between them? And how had she been so absolutely sure that you couldn't fall in love with someone you'd known for so long? That you'd have at least some idea it was going to happen within the first few minutes of meeting them?

As blindsiding as this was, it certainly felt like the kind of heartbreak that came from the end of a relationship with someone she had been completely in love with. She'd told Joe that the 'real thing' had a basis of genuine friendship but that there had to be chemistry involved. Well, they'd found that chemistry, hadn't they? It had just been too easy to dismiss the alchemy as 'fun' because they both knew there could never be a future together. Maggie wanted a family. Joe didn't. End of story.

Walking inside made Maggie come face to face with another part of what would be her new reality in about six months' time. Single parenthood. Laura looked tired. Worried.

'What's up?' Maggie asked.

'Harry's not feeling well. I'll have to keep him home from school tomorrow if he's not better but I can't afford to miss my shift...' Laura took a second glance at Maggie. 'Sorry... I shouldn't just dump on you like that, the moment you come through the door. You don't look like you've had the best day yourself.'

'It's okay.' It was actually a relief to have someone else to think about. 'What's the matter with Harry?'

'He's got a sore tummy and doesn't want to eat anything.'

'Any vomiting or diarrhoea?'

'Not yet.'

'Is he running a temperature?'

'I was just going to take it.'

'You do that,' Maggie said. 'I'll put the kettle on and make us a cup of tea.' Wine would be preferable, she thought, but that was off limits from now on. 'And don't worry about tomorrow. I've got some time off so I can look after Harry.'

'Really? I thought you'd only just started work for this week.'

'It's a long story. I'll tell you later.' Maggie poked her head around the kitchen door to wave at Harrison, who was lying on the couch, watching a cartoon on television. 'Hey, Harry…sorry you're not feeling well, buddy.'

His little face was pale beneath that thatch of dark spiky hair but he managed a brave grin as he waved back that melted Maggie's heart. He was such a cute kid and a delight to live with but Maggie knew she got to enjoy all the good bits and not have the responsibility of the other side of the coin, like childhood illnesses or injuries or the financial stress of being the sole provider. The world of single parenthood.

How had she ever contemplated going into that world voluntarily?

She could see just how terrifying it was going to be. Where was she going to live? How was she going to be able to afford everything she and the baby would need? How would she cope if the baby got really sick and she was all by herself?

Her future was not going to be anything like her fantasies of a big, happy family having picnics. She'd probably made it even less likely that she would ever find someone to share her life with. Look at Laura, who hadn't even been on a date in the last five years as far as Maggie knew.

Her flatmate came back into the kitchen with a thermometer in her hand. 'It's normal,' she said.

'That's good.'

'It's probably just a twenty four-hour bug of some kind. Or maybe he'll bounce back by tomorrow morning. Oh…thanks…' Laura reached for the mug of tea Maggie had made and then sat down at the table. 'Now…tell me what's going on with you.'

'Hmm…' Maggie sat down beside her. 'You'd better brace yourself…'

It was easy to pick up speed in this much wind.

Easy to hit the wave at just the perfect angle and push down with your legs and then jump and grip with your toes to roll the windward edge of the board to catch the wind and to bend your arms and knees to fly even higher.

Not so easy to keep the tail of the board in the right place so you didn't spin out when you touched down again on the choppy surface but Joe had done this a million times.

It never got old.

And it never failed to clear anything else out of his head. He just couldn't think about anything other than how to keep upright and sailing. He couldn't be aware of anything other than the chill and splash of the water, the rush of wind and the adrenaline spike of every jump and successful landing. The burn of tired muscles had to kick in at some point, of course, but it was almost dark by the time Joe finally hauled his gear across the beach to the car park.

The things he didn't want to think about were already creeping back by the time he was tying his board and sail onto his roof rack and it didn't help that going windsurfing had reminded him of being on the beach, not so long ago, with young Harry—another fatherless little boy like he'd been himself. Another reminder of just why he'd never, ever wanted to be in this situation. Having consumed so much physical energy by the windsurfing session, the raw emotional edges had blurred more than a little. But he still felt betrayed.

He was still too angry to ever want to speak to Maggie again. Joe cast a sideways glance at the familiar buildings as he drove past the Aratika Rescue Base on his way back into the central city and his apartment block. It was just as well that Don was forcing her to stand down for a few days and was removing her from front-line duties. Joe was nowhere near ready to see her again.

She'd used him. She'd probably been planning it ever since that day they'd delivered the baby with the shoulder dystocia. When she'd been carrying the kid and said, '*I think I want one...*' She'd asked him to be the sperm donor but then had just gone and done it despite him telling her exactly why it could never happen.

A stop at a red traffic light on a big intersection was long enough to let his thoughts throw a curveball into his anger. Okay, it was a bit of a coincidence that the fertile time of her cycle had just happened to be on a day they'd had the kind of job that almost never happened and Maggie had been close enough to hypothermia to have difficulty getting out of her uniform. She couldn't have actually planned that.

So it hadn't been entirely her fault, had it?

He hadn't dealt with those unexpected feelings of attraction towards Maggie and made sure that nothing ever happened. Worse, on that night in the shower room, he could have walked out. He could have kept walking so that they'd never opened that Pandora's box of sex between them. Or he could have, at the very least, gone to his locker, found his wallet and taken out that condom he always carried, just in case.

He'd been stupid.

It was no excuse that he'd trusted Maggie and believed her when she'd said it was safe. He had to take at least part of the blame.

Maggie got the rest of the blame.

The only one that couldn't be blamed was the new being that existed because of what had happened that night.

The baby.

His baby.

History was repeating itself. Two people who were entirely unsuited to be in a relationship were now bound to each other for ever as the parents of a child. An accidental pregnancy that would produce an unwanted child, like he had been.

No…that wasn't entirely true. Maggie wanted this baby. She was never going to tell that child that they had ruined her life. But Joe had a sudden flash of what her face had looked like earlier with tears rolling down her face. Her body language when she'd been standing beside her bike watching him leave with those slumped shoulders and air of defeat. She might have thought that a baby was what she wanted but she certainly wasn't too happy about finding out she had one on the way, was she?

So perhaps she hadn't planned it at all.

But it didn't actually matter now because it had happened and everything had changed.

He'd lost a friend he'd thought he could trust above anyone else.

He'd lost his colleague. There'd be no more shared excitement about getting dispatched to a challenge that was 'hot' enough to be a thrill.

He'd lost the freedom that had gone with an unencumbered future as well. Joe had no idea just how he was going to face up to the kind of responsibility of being a father but he wasn't about to repeat history and be the kind of man his own father had been. His own child was not going to grow up feeling like they didn't have a father.

It was too much loss for one day, he decided as he parked in the basement car park of his downtown apartment block. Too much change.

But it wasn't quite over.

The letter he pulled from his box in the foyer didn't get opened until Joe had showered off the sea water and had a nice, cold beer in front of him, but any comfort he was trying to give himself evaporated as he read the notice from his landlord.

This apartment block had been deemed an earthquake risk and needed urgent strengthening work.

Joe had little more than a month to find himself somewhere else to live.

He wasn't coming.

It was already fifteen minutes after the scheduled time for Maggie's appointment at the antenatal clinic for her first ultrasound examination.

She hadn't seen or spoken to Joe since she'd been stood down from her duties at the Aratika Rescue Base nearly two days ago. It was becoming automatic to check her phone repeatedly to see whether she might have missed a reply to the text she'd sent yesterday. She'd informed him of the results of her first appointment with an obstetrician that had confirmed what they already knew, and where and when this appointment for the first ultrasound was happening.

A part of Maggie was also clinging to the admittedly very faint hope that, somehow, the chaos of what was happening in both their lives would begin to settle down to a point where it might still be possible to salvage some of their friendship. They had to be able to talk to each other, didn't they? To make decisions about the future?

Not that Maggie expected anything from

Joe. She'd tried to make that clear when she'd finished the text she'd sent him yesterday.

I'm not telling you this because I expect you to be here. It's entirely your choice. It just feels wrong not to keep you in the loop.

'Margaret Lewis?' A technician came into the waiting area.

'That's me.' Maggie got to her feet, wincing a little at the discomfort her very full bladder was creating. 'I'm about to pop,' she told the technician. 'I hope I can last long enough.'

'You'll be fine.' The technician smiled. 'Most women forget about their bladders once they can see their babies. My name's Stella. Is your partner coming?'

'I…um… I'm not sure. He may have been held up.' Not that it felt accurate to refer to Joe as any kind of partner. She wasn't even working with him any more, let alone anything more personal. 'He's an air ambulance paramedic.'

'Oh, wow… That would be such an amazing job.'

'It is.'

And Maggie was missing being at work. Missing Joe. Grappling with the disturbing realisation that she'd fallen in love with someone who would only ever see her as a friend. Even though she had her flatmates around her at home, and Laura was being so sympathetic to her situation, Maggie was feeling very alone. Her mother had offered to travel to Wellington and come with her to this appointment but Maggie had declined the offer—just in case Joe decided he wanted to come. If he did, things would be tense enough without giving him the added pressure of being assessed by one of his child's grandparents.

'Okay…climb up on the bed here. We just need your tummy exposed. I'll tuck a towel over your clothes to protect them from the gel.'

'Ooh…that's cold…'

'It'll warm up in no time. Right…let's get started. I'll let you know what I'm doing as I go along. First up, I'm just going to check your ovaries and uterus and things like where the placenta is lying. Then we'll—' Stella broke off as there was a soft tap at the door. 'Yes?' she called.

The door opened a crack. 'They told me to come through,' a male voice said. 'Is that okay?'

Stella glanced at Maggie, who nodded,

even though her heart had just skipped a beat. 'That's Joe,' she said. 'My...the baby's father.'

He came into the room. 'Sorry I'm late,' he told Maggie. 'I had trouble finding somewhere to park.'

His gaze slid away from hers, which made Maggie think that maybe the difficulty hadn't had anything to do with finding a parking space and that it had actually been deciding whether he was going to come at all. It didn't matter. He was here now and... and it felt right.

Better than that, even.

'Stand behind the bed,' Stella told Joe. 'Close to Maggie's shoulder. That way you can both see what's happening on the screen.'

It felt really good to have him in the room. Maggie had to close her eyes for a moment to force back the prickle of tears. She had to clench her fists to remind herself that this wasn't anything like any fantasy she might have had about seeing her baby for the first time. Having the man she loved beside her sharing images that were all about their future together as a family.

That nobody was going to be holding her hand as this little miracle unfolded...

* * *

He almost hadn't come.

Joe had started to answer Maggie's text on a dozen or more occasions but, every time, he had deleted his messages before they got sent. Any words he chose felt stilted and couldn't come anywhere near expressing what he wanted to say—probably because he didn't actually *know* what he wanted to say.

He was still angry at being put into a position he had been so determined to never be in. He still felt betrayed. But mixed into those feelings was that determination not to be the man his own father had been. He was going to do better and that meant being somehow involved with his child's life right from the start. Starting with this examination that had actually taken quite a lot of courage to face up to.

Things were about to get very real.

'So we use the crown-rump length for dating,' Stella the technician said, as Joe took a deep breath and focussed on the screen of the ultrasound machine. 'It's the most accurate method, giving us a date to within five to seven days, but it's less useful after twelve weeks because the baby's starting to curl up by that stage.'

The images on the screen were just a blur of smudged black and white to Joe but Stella was pausing the cursor and clicking to make a mark before moving confidently to another point to repeat the process.

'I see the date for your last period would put you at about eleven weeks, but you had an episode of bleeding when you would have expected your next period?'

'More or less,' Maggie said quietly. 'But definitely a bit late. And, looking back, I was worried and then I was so relieved that I didn't think about it any more. It wasn't… um…it wasn't exactly planned…'

Joe clenched his jaw. That was an understatement. The tone of Maggie's voice echoed in his head for long moments after she'd stopped speaking. She sounded so unlike herself.

So subdued. As if she was having as much trouble as he was getting his head around this shocking development that was going to change his life for ever. Change both their lives but it was going to change Maggie's life far more than his because she was going to parent this child twenty-four seven. He would be a supportive but far more distant figure.

'These measurements confirm that,' Stella

told them. 'I'd put baby at eleven weeks, four days. Almost twelve. You're pretty much through your first trimester.'

Yes… Joe could feel the remnants of those shock waves.

He hadn't been wrong to trust Maggie. She really had believed that they were safe.

In silence, he kept watching the screen, taking a professional interest in the images that Stella explained to them both. The view of the four chambers of the heart was fascinating and it was getting easier to identify structures as they glimpsed organs like the bladder and kidneys. The long bones of the legs and the movements of joints had his eyes glued to the screen and then Stella changed the angle of the transducer and pressed it a little more deeply onto Maggie's abdomen.

'Oh…nice,' Stella murmured. 'We don't always get such a good 3D mug shot.'

And there it was. Their baby's face in such astonishing detail it felt like he could reach out and touch this newly forming little person.

His child…

Stella was taking a screenshot. Joe could imagine Maggie keeping a copy of that photo, Showing it to their child in years to come.

This was the very first time we saw you…

Something very unexpected was happening for Joe right now. He had come here prepared to put his hand up to take responsibility and be part of his child's life. What he hadn't anticipated at all was that he was going to feel…so connected. So emotional. He was swallowing a rather large lump in his throat as Stella finished up her examination and moved the transducer again. They got a final, and poignant, glimpse of the baby.

The bottom of a single foot, with each tiny toe clearly visible.

'Cute.' Stella smiled. 'Let's get a picture of that, too.'

And then it was over and Maggie was walking through the corridors of the Royal's maternity suite's outpatient department, holding an envelope that contained several black and white images.

Joe walked beside her. The silence between them felt odd but not hostile.

'Can I buy you a coffee?' he asked.

He saw the flash of surprise in her eyes. Wariness, even. But then Maggie gave a soft huff of laughter. 'Maybe a tea?'

'Oh, sorry… I forgot.'

'That's okay. You've had a lot on your mind.'

'Yeah…'

Instead of taking a table in the small café in the hospital's foyer, Joe bought their drinks in takeaway cups and they went outside to a courtyard area away from the main entrance, where there were plenty of bench seats and a small garden with a fountain.

For a while, they sat side by side in silence. It was Maggie that broke it.

'I really am sorry, Joe. This isn't your fault and I feel really bad because I know how much you didn't want it.'

'It is partly my fault,' he said. 'It does take two to tango.'

His choice of words reminded him of dancing with Maggie. Of how solid their friendship had seemed, the night of Fizz and Cooper's wedding, when he'd told her stuff about his childhood he'd never told anyone else. It also reminded him of holding her in his arms when they hadn't been dancing and of how good the sex had been. No, not good. Totally, unbelievably amazing.

So what if they weren't in love or they'd never had any intention of being in a 'real' relationship? They had so many things in common, didn't they?

Including a baby now. Maggie had put down her cup to open the envelope and she'd pulled out one of the photos. The one of that tiny foot.

'It's so real now,' she said softly. 'I know it's not what we wanted and I know it's going to be tough but…you know what?'

Joe nodded slowly. He knew exactly what. 'You already love this baby.'

'Yeah…'

'I'm going to be here for you. For him… or her…' Joe gently touched the foot in the photograph with his fingertip. 'We can do this together. Like the "dream team".'

'You don't want that, Joe.'

'Actually, I think I do.' Joe turned to meet Maggie's gaze. 'I came here today because I was determined to be a better man than my father was but right now I can understand what he was trying to do and…maybe it would have worked if my mother had actually wanted me. If she had loved me from the moment she first saw me, like you do with this baby.'

Maggie was looking bewildered. 'Maybe what would have worked?'

'Their marriage. Being able to provide a happy home for their kid. For me.'

Her eyes widened. 'Are you saying what I think you're saying?'

Joe swallowed hard. And then he nodded.

'Yes. I want to be part of this baby's life. Part of your life. We could be a family, Maggie, and I think… I think we could make it work.'

She was staring at him and Joe could see that she had tears in her eyes. Happy tears? He took a deep breath and forced his lips into a smile.

'Marry me,' he said.

CHAPTER EIGHT

IT WAS ON the tip of her tongue to say yes.

How stupid was that?

Part of her didn't think so. The part that included her heart, which was squeezing itself so hard at the moment because when you were in love with someone, what you wanted to hear more than anything else was that they were prepared to commit to a lifetime together.

But the other part of Maggie that included her head was dismissing it in no uncertain terms and it was her head that directed her words.

'You've got to be kidding,' she said to Joe. 'You, of all people, should know that getting married just because you've got a baby on the way is a totally stupid thing to do. For everybody involved, but most especially for the baby.'

She could see the flash of agreement——or

maybe it was relief— —in his eyes but he was frowning as well. Was he as conflicted as Maggie felt?

'But this is different,' he said.

'How?'

'We're such good friends. We've known each other for years. We *like* each other...'

The squeeze on Maggie's heart tightened enough to be painful. 'Like' was not a word she would use to describe how she felt about Joe. She couldn't tell him that, of course. About how much she was missing him already? About how wrong she'd been to think she would never want to be anything more than friends with him? How vulnerable would you make yourself by doing that? And how crushing would it be to get reminded that he could never feel that way about her. It was kind of like having to hide those first flickers of sexual attraction because revealing them might have damaged what they had in a special friendship.

Maggie's breath came out in a sigh. It was beyond damaged now, wasn't it? That old, safe friendship with no complications had been blown to smithereens.

'I love you, Maggie, you know that, don't you? We're best mates.'

'Yeah…' Maggie pressed her lips together to stop herself saying anything else.

Being prepared to commit to a lifetime together wasn't actually the thing you wanted to hear most of all when you were in love with someone, she realised. The top of that list would be the three little words Joe had just said to her. Except he had qualified them. Diluted them into something that wasn't enough.

Could never be enough.

Maggie could never marry anyone who hadn't fallen into the crazy, overwhelming space that she was in, preferably at exactly the same moment. The moment when they both just knew that this was 'it'. That they had found their person. You *fell* in love, everybody knew that. You weren't friends with someone for years and years and then just woke up one day and realised that you were head over heels in love, having somehow slipped sideways into that state without noticing it happening.

So maybe what Maggie was feeling for Joe was just something to do with pregnancy hormones. Or the ripple effect from the emotional bond she was developing with this baby she had been unknowingly carrying for so long already. Whatever. Her head was in a mess. So was her heart.

'I understand why you think it might be a good idea,' she said slowly. 'But you've actually been there, remember? You felt like your parents' miserable marriage was your fault.'

'Maybe ours wouldn't be miserable. We enjoy each other's company. We work together well. Hey...we're the—'

'Don't say it,' Maggie warned. 'Can you hear yourself? Saying that being friends and being able to work together as some kind of "dream team" is a good enough reason to get married? Don't you want more than that from someone you're going to hopefully spend the rest of your life with? Something like romance? Passion, even? Because I sure do.'

She slotted the photographs back into their envelope.

'I'm not going to shut you out, Joe,' she added. 'You're this baby's father and you can be as much a part of his or her life as you want to be, but I'm not going to marry you. I'm not going to marry anyone who isn't as much in love with me as I am with him.'

Oh, help...did that sound like a confession? No, it was just a general statement. Maggie wasn't even sure she could trust the notion that she *was* in love with Joe any more given that it could just be crazy hormones. It was Joe himself who'd said that hormones always wore off. He might have been talking about the kind of hormones involved with falling in love, but surely pregnancy hormones didn't last the whole nine months?

She needed time, anyway. She had barely started getting her head around the fact that she was going to become a mother. Sorting out how she really felt about Joe might need to go on the back burner, although the idea that they could salvage the foundation of their friendship was very welcome.

Joe seemed to be in agreement.

'Fair enough,' he said. 'And you're right. As usual…'

The smile didn't look as forced this time—the way it had when he'd proposed to her. It looked like a smile she'd seen on Joe's face countless times. A genuine, warm smile.

The smile she loved. How could she not smile right back?

It was so good to see a smile on Maggie's face again.

She'd looked so upset the last time he'd seen her, in that shocking confrontation when he had found out he was going to become a father. Today, in the dim light of the ultrasound room, she'd looked flat—as if she'd had the stuffing knocked out of her. And she'd looked so wary when he'd offered to buy her a coffee. Had she expected him to have another go at her?

Another unexpected thing had happened when he'd been looking at those images of the baby. Not just the feeling of being connected and close to tears and wanting to protect that tiny being. Maybe it had been the wash of how powerful those feelings were that had made any residual anger about all of this fade enough to seem insignificant.

He hadn't been betrayed. He believed Maggie had genuinely thought they were safe. And accidents happened. This could have happened with any of the women who'd been part of his life in the past and, if anything, he was lucky that it had happened with Maggie. Other women might have expected—demanded, even—the public commitment of marriage, but it was the last thing that Maggie wanted and she was right.

They'd known all along that they weren't meant to be life partners. Joe had to admit that the offer had been impulsive. He had personal experience of exactly what kind of fallout there could be from using an accidental pregnancy as a good reason to get married. He was relieved that Maggie had turned him down. It felt like a lot of pressure had just been lifted off his shoulders.

It wasn't unusual to co-parent these days without being in any kind of relationship with the other parent and if they were on friendly terms that had to be immeasurably easier. He and Maggie had been very good friends and this smile they were sharing now felt like the first step back to that friendship.

'I'd be bad husband material, anyway.' Joe's smile faded. 'I'm going to be homeless pretty soon if I don't get on with finding a new place to live.'

'What? What's happened to your apartment?'

'The building's being emptied. They've got to do some major strengthening. It's been identified as an earthquake risk.'

'We've got a spare room at the flat. We still haven't found a replacement for Cooper. If you get desperate, I'm sure everybody would be happy if you used the room. Until you found a place of your own.'

'Hmm…' Joe glanced sideways at Maggie. Those last words had revealed that Maggie had made the offer before she'd really thought through any consequences.

It could be very awkward. The reminder of the physical relationship they hadn't actually officially ended would be there between them all the time. And, okay, it probably was over now but that wouldn't stop the memories, would it?

Those flashes of sensation—one of which Joe was experiencing right now—that reminded him of just how amazing sex with Maggie was. Oh, man…he felt guilty for even thinking about that when there were far more important things he should be facing. Like taking responsibility for the child he had fathered. Like finding himself somewhere to live.

'I think it's fate,' he told Maggie. 'I'm thirty-seven. I've been saving money for a long time without making a sensible investment. Maybe it's time I bought a real house. Something a bit more child-friendly than an apartment, anyway. With a garden, perhaps?'

Did Maggie realise that he was talking about something more than simply a house? It was difficult to try and explain something he didn't understand himself, though. Those feelings during that ultrasound. That he'd understood that Maggie already loved this baby because…he'd felt at least something similar to that himself. 'And a swing,' he added, his voice cracking just a little. 'For…when this kid comes to visit his dad, you know?'

Maggie was silent for a long moment. When she finally raised her gaze to meet Joe's he'd never seen an expression like that on her face before. It looked like total amazement, laced with…hope? Excitement? Except that there was something else there as well. Something that made him want to hug her and tell her that everything was going to be okay.

He'd seen Maggie's face glowing plenty of times but not like this. As if her normal confidence was nowhere to be found. As if she was stepping onto new ground and it was scary and she couldn't quite believe that someone was offering to keep her company.

Joe wanted to do more than keep Maggie company. He wanted to keep her safe.

It felt perfectly natural to put his arm around her shoulders and pull her sideways for a quick hug.

'We'll work this out,' he said. 'Together. You'll see.'

'So I don't have to be stuck in the basement with Danny, helping out with supplies all the time. I'm allowed to use one of the SUVs for first response if the base gets asked for assistance. I just have to wait for backup for any lifting.' Maggie sighed as she poured hot water over the tea bag in her mug in Aratika's staffroom. 'I told Don I'd be much happier on a bike. It's so much quicker to get through traffic that way.'

'Are you still riding your bike?' Cooper sounded surprised as he looked up from where he was peering over Joe's shoulder at the screen of his phone.

'Don't go there,' Joe warned. 'I tried suggesting that it might not be such a good idea last week and I got my head bitten off.'

'Oh, sorry... I wasn't thinking.' Cooper turned back to the phone. 'I got the same lecture from Fizz. Pregnancy is not an illness. Women can work until they go into labour if that's what they want to do. Aye... that one, mate.' He reached forward to point at the screen. 'It looks awesome.'

'My obstetrician says I can carry on with anything that I normally do.' Maggie kept her tone level. She had enough changing in her life right now without being pressured to give up her beloved bike just yet. 'That I'll know when it's time to stop because it's getting uncomfortable. Apart from the heavy lifting, of course.'

'And keeping out of the way of any aggressive patients,' Joe muttered. 'Or hazardous accident scenes.'

Cooper chuckled. 'You're getting onto thin ice. Maggie's sensible. You can trust her judgement.'

'True.' Joe looked up and Maggie couldn't help her breath catching as those warm hazel eyes captured her own gaze. Since they'd shared that appointment for the first ultrasound examination of their baby, they had been tentatively restoring their friendship, step by step—hopefully along with the trust that had been implicit.

Not the extra, physical side that had been added into that friendship, of course. How could they, when it was the reason they were both facing a very different future from the one they might have been expecting? But it was a good start. They could talk to each other at work, even though that currently seemed to consist of Maggie demanding every detail of the more interesting cases Joe had been deployed to, usually with one of the HEMS doctors like Tom or Adam as his crew partner.

He'd had a job yesterday where a hunter had fallen down a steep bank onto rocks in thick forest in the Rimutaka Ranges.

'Why couldn't you winch in to the scene? Was it too windy?'

'How far did you have to walk? Did you have any help to carry the gear?'

'You had to abseil down to the patient? Wow...how did that go?'

'What else did you find on the secondary survey? Did he have abdominal as well as chest injuries?'

'So how did you deal with the failed intubation attempt? Did you try more padding to adjust the positioning? How fast was the swelling obscuring what you could see?'

Joe understood how much Maggie was missing being on the front line and it was becoming their new normal—to have a debrief even though Maggie hadn't been to the job, the way they would have if they'd managed the case together.

'Yeah, I had to use padding to get the earlobe in line with the sternal notch but it was difficult. It was getting dark already and we were down a cliff in the middle of a forest. Maybe we should have considered a tracheostomy earlier. It was touch and go there for a while. What would you have done?'

Right now, the expression in Joe's eyes suggested that he would welcome her opinion on something else.

'So…come and see what you think of this house,' he said. 'It's up on the hill. Not far from where Cooper and Fizz live.'

'It's a great suburb.' Cooper nodded. 'There's a good crèche nearby and a primary school. We've got it all sussed.'

Maggie stepped forward to look at the images Joe was scrolling through on a real estate website. She had to resist the urge to lean close enough to be touching his shoulder or to let a stray curl of his hair brush her cheek.

These waves of longing had to be controlled until her wayward hormones had settled down and the swirls of confusion had cleared and she could totally believe that she wasn't in love with him. It was enough for now that Joe was no longer angry with her. That he believed she hadn't deliberately set out to get pregnant and that he was willing to become involved as a responsible parent.

Except it didn't feel like enough. The confused part of Maggie's head—and heart—was telling her that she wanted more. That she was fighting a losing battle by pretending it was something temporary that would wear off soon. And those messages were in conflict with others that were reminding her that Joe would definitely not want more. That the fragility of the new relationship they were forging would be very easy to damage and that new damage on top of the recent trauma would spell the end of any trust between them.

She focussed on the screen. The house being advertised for sale was an old weatherboard villa with a big veranda wrapping around two sides of the house and a room with a turret on the corner.

'It's gorgeous,' she said. 'Like a little castle. But it's *huge*...'

'It's divided into two flats,' Joe said. 'Which means I could rent half of it out which will help pay the mortgage.'

'The harbour view's amazing.'

'And the garden. Look at that.'

'Bit of work there,' Cooper warned. 'Do you really want to spend your days off mowing lawns and weeding gardens? When will you find time for your windsurfing?'

Maggie couldn't miss the slight hesitation before Joe spoke. 'Things change,' he said quietly. 'And sometimes the new things are worth giving up other stuff for.'

Was that a doubtful note she detected in his voice? Sad, even? No...it sounded more like Joe was getting used to the big changes to his life that were coming. That he was prepared to embrace them. Mind you, it was hard to imagine him giving up the freedom of skimming waves to be that domesticated.

'It's a lot different to your modern apartment,' she said. 'Old houses take a lot more housework. And maintenance.'

'Looks in pretty good nick to me. It's been rewired. And painted.'

'Photos can be very deceptive. You've learned that much in a couple of weeks' house-hunting, surely?'

Joe grunted. 'I'm running out of time. You know what?' He tapped the screen. 'I'm going to call the agent and set up a viewing. Come with me, Maggie.'

'Why?'

'Because you're good to talk about things with. Bounce ideas off. And I can trust your judgement, that's why.'

'Management of the case of a house instead of a patient? With an extensive debrief?'

Joe's smile told her she had hit the nail on the head. 'You up for it?'

'Sure.'

Maggie kept her tone light but that confusing swirl of messages and feelings ramped up a notch. She couldn't let Joe recognise the magnetic pull that made the prospect of spending time alone with him so compelling but she almost resented the sensible part of her brain that was warning her this might not be a good idea. That she could be putting roadblocks or, at the very least, diversions in the way of sorting out what her real feelings were and how she was going to deal with them. Surely spending more time with Joe was exactly what would help to sort the mess in her head and her heart?

'This definitely sounds like a project that needs the attention of the "dream team",' she added jokingly. 'Just let me know where and when.'

The house was beautiful.

With polished wooden floors, high ceilings with ornate plasterwork and rooms big enough to seem totally indulgent by modern standards, it was a glorious example of an early New Zealand villa.

And Maggie had fallen in love with it the moment she'd walked through the heavy, wooden front door with its stained-glass panels. Tall sash windows made every room light enough to see the patches of peeling paint on the ceilings and the deep scratches and marks from years of high-heeled shoes, dogs' nails and probably children's toys on

the floorboards. The signs of a house that
had been well lived in. A family home...

A big family home. The kind you could
have fitted six children in before it had been
divided into two apartments. The kind of
home that Maggie could have imagined in
those days of dreaming about a large family—right down to a dog or two.

'You could have a dog,' she found herself
telling Joe. 'How cool would that be?'

He didn't look excited by the idea. 'It's
not fair to keep a dog if you're working full
time,' he said. 'I wouldn't want the responsibility.'

Maggie turned away to look at the view
from the enormous bay window in this huge
sitting room. It was similar to the view that
Cooper and Fizz had from their small villa,
with a lovely glimpse of Wellington Harbour
in the distance. She could actually see a helicopter gaining height as it came from the
direction of the Aratika Rescue Base. Who
was on board? she wondered. And what kind
of adrenaline rush would the challenge produce? Would it be what she and Joe might
consider a 'hot' one? She missed the intensity of that work. She even missed the long
days and the sometimes exhausting physical challenges. Joe was right, though. You

couldn't do a job like that with its twelve-hour or more shifts and leave a dog at home alone.

But if a dog was a responsibility that Joe didn't want, how did he really feel about a child being in his near future? It was still too early to feel this baby moving inside her, but Maggie put her hand on her belly anyway—her fingers spread a little as if she needed to protect it.

'So this half of the house has the view. I have to say it's one of the best I've seen in a very long time.' The real estate agent had been enthusiastically drawing their attention to every detail of the house from the moment they'd entered. 'I imagine you'd choose this half to live in and rent the other half out? I've got an estimate of the kind of income you could expect to make from doing that, if you want to look at it, Joe?'

'Yes…thank you.' Joe went to stand beside the agent to look at the clipboard she was holding.

'It's lucky that both apartments are empty at the moment. You could get possession very fast if your offer was acceptable. I understand you're in a bit of a hurry?'

'Mmm…' Joe had flipped a page on the

clipboard. 'So these are the floor plans? The second apartment looks smaller.'

'It still has two bedrooms and a good-sized sitting room that was originally another bedroom, I believe. Or maybe a library. You could easily knock through and take it back to its former glory as a large family home.' The agent sent a smile in Maggie's direction. 'How perfect would that be for when you guys want to start your family?'

'We're not a couple,' Maggie told her, surprising herself with a tone that was uncharacteristically rude. It wasn't that the agent needed to know. It was more like a stab of disappointment that had prompted her to say something. She and Joe might be having a baby together but they weren't starting any kind of 'real' family. It was more than disappointing. It felt heartbreaking enough to tell Maggie that her hormonal imbalance was nowhere near settling down. Good grief… there was something about the agent's words, or this house-viewing business, that almost had her on the verge of tears.

'We're just friends,' she added, trying to make her tone friendlier. 'I'm here to provide a feminine viewpoint, that's all.'

'Oh… I beg your pardon…' The agent's cheeks went pink. 'Well…how 'bout I leave you to have a look at the bedrooms and bathroom on this side and then I'll meet you in the other apartment? That'll give you a bit of time to talk about things.'

Maggie walked closer to the windows to stare down at the garden. There was a lovely patch of lawn before the slope merged into a grove of trees. She could see a path leading somewhere and an old tyre swing hanging from the large tree branch. She could also feel Joe moving towards her.

'Just friends?' he asked quietly.

Maggie swallowed hard. 'What would you call us, then?'

'I don't know.' Joe blew out a breath. 'Definitely friends, but there's something bigger now as well, don't you think? We're going to be parents together.'

'Not exactly together.'

'You know what I mean. We're both going to be the parents of the same baby. It feels… more than "just friends".'

'Yeah…' It was Maggie's turn to sigh. 'It's certainly more complicated than it used to be.'

The silence felt awkward.

'I *love* this house,' Maggie said brightly, to try and change the subject. 'It needs work but it feels like it would be a lovely place to live.'

'I love it, too.' Joe nodded. 'And...you know what? It could be perfect—for both of us.'

Startled, Maggie turned her head swiftly, her eyes widening as she looked up at Joe. 'What are you talking about?'

'It's just occurred to me that this could be the ideal solution.'

'Solution to what?'

'To being co-parents but not together.'

'I still have no idea what you're talking about.'

'This house has two sides. Part of the same house but separate. Imagine if I lived on one side and you lived on the other?'

Her mind jumped to that scenario with remarkable ease. She would see Joe every day. They would be a part of each other's lives. They could share meals together, maybe, and gardening chores. Almost like a real family. She could actually see herself out there in a couple of years, harvesting some vegetables from the garden, and she could see Joe push that tyre swing with a toddler sitting inside it, shrieking with glee. In the periphery of that flash of fantasy, Maggie could even see the waving tail of a happy dog. A golden retriever, perhaps...

But there was something else, too. Someone else? Joe's latest girlfriend, probably. She would see him bringing new ones home. Ringing in the changes because they'd got too close and wanted more than he was prepared to give. He might tell her about it over a glass of wine in the evening—because she was his friend. A good friend. The mother of his child, in fact, but still only a friend.

She couldn't do it. Because it would be nothing like a real family. She would be close to Joe but there was a very real possibility that she would feel even lonelier than she did at the moment. Wanting to be with him. Wanting to touch and be touched by Joe. Maggie could feel herself welling up with that new twinge of longing. Oh, boy... There was still no sign of the effects of these new hormones wearing off. If anything, they were getting more powerful.

'You okay?' Joe's voice was concerned.

'Mmm...' Maggie fought for control, focussing on the view again.

'You hate the idea, don't you?'

'I...um...think it might make things too difficult.'

'I thought it would make things easier. As far as sharing the parenting, anyway.'

'I'm sure it would,' Maggie murmured. 'But...it might be *too* close, you know?'

'Not sure I do.' Joe was frowning. 'We've stopped seeing each other like that, haven't we? It was a mistake to mess up our friendship with sex. And…you were very clear about not wanting to marry me and I agree that it needs more than a basis of friendship to make that kind of commitment, so…that's the end of that, isn't it?'

Maggie needed to agree with him. She tried to nod her head but it wasn't quite working. She did tilt her head up to start the movement but all that did was let her gaze snag on Joe's and she could see that he was thinking about exactly what she was thinking about.

'Oh… *Maggie*…'

His voice was a low rumble laced with desire. He lifted his hand to lay his palm gently against her cheek and Maggie felt her eyes drifting shut as she leaned into the touch. She couldn't see Joe's head slowly dipping but she could feel the heat of his skin becoming more intense as he closed the distance between their faces. And then she was aware of only the electric tingle as his lips covered hers, moving over them so slowly, so tenderly, it was utterly heartbreaking.

'Oh…don't mind me…'

The cheerful voice of the real estate agent

felt like someone was throwing a bucket of cold water in their direction. They both jerked apart.

'I wondered what was taking you so long,' the agent continued. The knowing smile on her face suggested that she knew any earlier embarrassment had been misplaced. 'I see you are…um…pretty *good* friends.'

It was Maggie's cheeks that had gone pink this time. She couldn't meet the agent's gaze. She couldn't look at Joe, either.

'So…do you want to look at the other apartment?'

Maggie could feel Joe's gaze on her. Willing her to look up again. Wanting to know whether she was interested in the opportunity this house could provide of living so closely together while they co-parented their child.

She forced herself to look up. To meet his gaze and shake her head just enough to relay the information that she couldn't do it. That the kiss they'd just shared had made things even more complicated and it wouldn't be a good idea for anybody involved here.

It seemed that he understood. Given the swift way his gaze slid away from Maggie's, it also seemed that he was either regretting that kiss or he was also feeling confused about how to define their relationship—or lack of it.

'I don't think we need to see the other apartment at the moment,' he told the agent.

'Oh…' She sounded disappointed. 'So you're not interested in the house, then?'

'On the contrary.'

Joe's voice was clipped. He was going into his efficient mode, Maggie realised, sounding like he did when he had a patient in critical condition and it was a race against time to save a life. He was in charge and he was going to make something happen.

'I love the house,' Joe added, seeming to grow an inch or two taller as he straightened his spine. 'I'll come back tomorrow and bring someone who can assess the condition of the place properly but I'll certainly be putting an offer in. As soon as possible.'

CHAPTER NINE

'I HEAR YOU'VE gone and bought a house, Joe.'

'Yep. The contract went unconditional yesterday. I take possession in a couple of weeks.'

Joe was restocking a drug roll, sliding ampoules into the row of tiny pockets. Fentanyl, ketamine, morphine… He itemised the drugs on the record sheet, signed his name against the entry and then handed the sheet to his partner for the additional signature. He was working with Tom Chapman today, the specialist consultant in the emergency department of the Royal who had begun working at Aratika when Fizz had had to give up her air rescue shifts.

'Exciting.' Tom nodded. 'From what Andy said, it sounds like a big place.'

'It's an old house. Divided into two apartments. Hey…you're not looking for somewhere new to live by any chance, are you?'

Tom laughed. 'No. And I like my little apartment. Easy to clean and maintain. Boring but very practical.' He shook his head, still grinning. 'Bit like me, really.'

Joe chuckled. He hadn't worked with Tom that often yet and knew nothing about his private life but he had always been impressed with this experienced doctor's ability to stay calm in any emergency and deal with it in a confident and highly skilled manner. Okay, he didn't smile that often and there was something very serious in his gaze a lot of the time but he had an absolute passion for his work and it was obvious that he cared very much for every patient he worked on.

'Hmm.' Joe continued gathering other supplies like the small, foil packages containing alcohol wipes, plastic packages with Luer plugs and a roll of tape, but he flicked Tom a sideways glance. 'You're not boring, mate, but you're probably a lot more sensible than me. I may well find I've bitten off more than I can chew, house-wise. Don't know what got into me.'

'You must have fallen in love with the place.'

'Nah…' Joe shook his head. 'I don't fall in love with women so it's not likely to happen with a house. It's a good investment, that's all.'

Except that a nice, practical little apartment like Tom had might have been an even better investment. Why had he made up his mind on the spot like that and then followed through with a second viewing and negotiating an agreed price? Because he had the thought lurking in the back of his mind that he might be able to persuade Maggie that the separate but close living arrangements could really work?

Or was it because it felt like a real home? A real family home. The kind where you could have a Sunday roast for lunch. He'd looked at that old swing in the tree in the garden and imagined what it would be like growing up in that house as a kid. A kid who felt wanted—the way he was determined that his child would always feel. The way he'd never felt himself, as a child. A kid with two parents, even, and it was a shock to realise that he could so easily see himself and Maggie as those loving parents. To imagine them loving each other as well as their child...

There were feelings being stirred that Joe had never wanted to revisit. Disturbing emotional currents that he had no idea how to deal with. It wasn't just to do with the baby, either. It had been a big mistake to kiss Maggie again. That had been lurking in the back of his mind for the last few weeks as well. Haunting his dreams and interfering with his focus too frequently to be acceptable. The softness of her lips. The warmth and smell and *taste* of her…

It was impossible to remember that kiss and not have his mind open a door that let his thoughts sneak off into the memories of what it had been like to kiss Maggie Lewis a lot more thoroughly. To feel the shape of her body beneath his hands and his lips. To be able to laugh, even, as sexual play led to the kind of release that had been a complete revelation for Joe.

He shouldn't be thinking about it at all but he couldn't really identify those feelings that were being stirred up and therefore had no idea how to fix his confusion. It didn't help that there was so much more he had to think about now that his future was moving in a direction he hadn't wanted to consider. The future that featured himself as a father.

It wasn't just that he was missing the sex. If that was all there was to it, it would have been easy enough in the last few weeks to have reconnected with an old girlfriend, perhaps, or find someone new. Instinct was still telling him, very firmly, that that kind of hook-up would not solve anything, no matter how good the sex might be. If anything, it would probably make it harder to sort out what was going on in his head, which was quite confusing enough already.

And maybe Maggie was feeling the same kind of confusion. Maybe that was why she seemed to have been deliberately avoiding spending any time alone with him ever since that house viewing. Was she missing him in anything like the same way he was missing her?

At least it was always possible to shut off any of those thoughts when he was actually involved in any kind of patient care but times like this, out of work hours or on station between missions, it seemed impossible to stop his thought processes getting hijacked. What he should be thinking about right now was making sure he had everything available in his kit that might be needed on the next critical case they were called to. He put more effort into focussing.

'Do we need any laryngeal mask airways?' Tom called, from the other side of the storage room.

'Yes. Grab a size four and five.' It was always good to have extras of the sizes they used the most often.

Tom handed him the airway devices. 'Anything else?'

'I think we're done. Let's see if we can get a coffee upstairs before we get another call.'

Both men paused as they walked past the windows that overlooked the helipad. Andy and Nick were still busy cleaning the chopper after the last mission they'd been on that had involved a fair bit of bodily fluids getting splashed around. Dark grey clouds were gathering in the sky above and a few raindrops pelted the windows and trickled down the glass.

'We're going to get some more accidents with this weather front coming in,' Tom said. 'The wind was bad enough without adding in the rain.'

'We did good at the last one,' Joe reminded him. 'I didn't think we'd get her into ED alive. That was a nasty smash. Vans can be hard to control in a high wind.'

Tom nodded slowly. 'They're the best jobs,' he said quietly. 'When you know for sure that the time saved and what we can offer in the way of pre-hospital medicine is what really made the difference between life and death. That some police officer isn't on his way to knock on someone's door and deliver the news that life, as they know it, is over.'

Wow… Tom really could get serious at times. Joe couldn't think of anything to say as they carried on into the staffroom to be greeted by a cheerful voice.

'You boys are just in time. My banana cake got cool enough to ice while you were out. And I've put some whipped cream in the middle. Sit yourselves down for five minutes.'

'It's you who should be sitting down for five minutes, Shirley. You never stop.'

'I feel better than I have in years.' Shirley was beaming as she set plates with large wedges of cake on them in front of Joe and Tom. 'Twenty years younger, in fact. Have you seen Maggie anywhere? She loves my banana cake.'

'It's her day off,' Joe told her. 'I think she was going up the coast to visit her parents.'

'Is she going to move back home?' Shirley asked. 'When that baby arrives?'

'Not that I know of.'

Surely Maggie would have said something if she was considering moving out of the city? Her parents were a good ninety minutes' drive away. But then again, why would she say anything? They were friends, not life partners. Living in a different town didn't mean that they couldn't co-parent. It would just make it a lot more difficult. On the opposite end of the spectrum he had suggested with the idea that Maggie could live in the second apartment of that old house he'd just bought.

Shirley put mugs and a pot of coffee in front of the men. Her glance made Joe feel like she could see far more than he might be comfortable with.

'Has Maggie seen that new house of yours?'

Yep. Seemed like Shirley really was telepathic to some degree. 'She came with me.'

'It's got two apartments, I hear.'

Joe sighed. 'Yep. And, yes, before you ask, Shirley, I did suggest that Maggie move into one of them. She said she didn't want to. That things were complicated enough already.'

Shirley echoed his sigh and then tutted with disappointment as she went back towards a sink that was full of her baking and mixing dishes. She might have been muttering something about people not seeing things that were right under their noses but Joe pretended not to hear.

He stared at the slice of cake on his plate. 'I actually asked Maggie to marry me,' he confessed to Tom.

Good grief…why on earth had he said that to someone he didn't know that well? Because Tom was so calm and sensible that he might have some advice to offer? Maybe it was because he wasn't as close a friend yet as someone like Andy. Or Cooper, who was still bathing in the rosy glow of both marriage with someone he was very much in love with and the excitement of expecting his first child.

'She said no, I take it?'

'She thinks there's got to be more than friendship. That you've got to be in love.'

Tom ate a bite of cake slowly and then nodded. 'She's right.'

Joe tried to eat some cake in the silence that followed, punctuated only by Shirley banging cake tins in the background, but it was hard to swallow.

'I wouldn't know about that,' he said. 'Like I said, I've never been in love that I know of. With a house *or* a person.'

Because he'd never let himself get past those roadblocks?

'You'd know, if you were,' Tom told him.

'How?'

Tom shrugged. 'Everything's different. It's like the sun has just been turned on in your personal universe. Everything's so much brighter. Warmer.'

Joe stared at his colleague. There were certainly depths to this man that he had never recognised. 'You've been there?'

'Yeah…' Tom's smile was slow. Poignant. 'Past tense is right, unfortunately. I lost my wife and son in a car accident a few years ago now.'

'Oh… *God*… I'm so sorry. I had no idea.' Joe caught his breath. No wonder Tom felt so strongly about the kind of job they'd just been on when they'd saved the life of a young woman who'd crashed her car. No wonder he seemed so serious at times.

'It's okay.' Tom drained his coffee mug. 'You're not the only one with no idea. It's not something I talk about. It broke me but I've put my life back together. I know I couldn't do it again but I also know that you'll know when it happens to you. And that for a marriage to work, it needs to happen on both sides.'

And that was never going to happen. Maggie had made it clear right from the start that she would never feel like that about him. Joe wasn't in love with Maggie—he couldn't be—but he did miss her. He missed the easy friendship. He missed the sex, too, of course, but it didn't feel as if his personal universe had been plunged into darkness. It just felt different.

Emptier.

And because he wasn't in love with Maggie and she wasn't in love with him, Tom was in agreement that she'd been right in refusing to marry him. That meant she would probably be making the right choice if she chose to move away from the city to raise her child with the help of her parents.

Without him.

This new emptiness of his personal universe kicked up a notch or two. Joe reached for another forkful of his cake in the hope of filling a tiny portion of that emptiness but he didn't get the chance to sink his teeth into it. His pager sounded.

So did Tom's.

'Bike versus truck,' Tom announced. 'I knew we'd be in for a spate of accidents this afternoon.'

Andy already had the rotors going by the time the two men had picked up their kits and helmets and were climbing aboard.

'Got cleaned up in the nick of time,' he said. 'Buckle up, it's getting a bit wild out there and we're heading into the worst of it, up the coast.'

It was a ten-minute ride, buffeted by wind. Things seemed noisier than usual and their information was coming in by crackled sound bites. A motorbike had skidded on the newly wet tarmac and had been clipped by a truck on a corner. One person was unhurt, another was reported as Status Two, which meant that they were unstable and potentially seriously injured. Visibility was less than perfect with rain streaking the Perspex and landing on a section of the road that the police and fire service had cleared for them took all of Andy's skill along with the backup of the medical crew watching out for hazards.

'Clear this side,' Tom confirmed.

'Tail clear,' Joe added.

Droplets of water on Joe's helmet visor were intensifying the colours of the flashing lights of emergency vehicles as he strode, ahead of Tom, to the centre of the accident scene. Red and blue flashes from a police car and an ambulance. He could see that the cab of the truck was empty so the driver had got out. That was probably him sitting in the back of the ambulance with a policewoman beside him.

Joe could also see the wheels of the motorbike, which was lying on its side just in front of a cluster of crouching people that was obscuring his view of their patient.

'Air Rescue,' he called. 'Let me through...'

People shifted. Joe could see the feet of their patient poking out from beneath a blanket. A paramedic was focussed on whatever she was hearing through her stethoscope and another was pulling an oxygen mask from its packaging. Two fire officers were holding up a tarpaulin both to keep rain off the injured person and shield them from curious stares from onlookers. From the corner of his eye, as he stepped forward, Joe was taking in the damage to the motorbike as an indication of how serious this accident had been.

It still looked largely intact, which was a good sign but no guarantee that the rider might have escaped a critical injury. The only damage Joe could see was that a handlebar was bent and the paintwork was pretty scratched. Sky-blue paintwork, he registered. Unusual.

The same as Maggie's motorbike.

He took another step forward, aware of the chill running down his spine, and then he stopped so abruptly that Tom bumped into the kit on his back.

'No...' Joe could feel the blood draining from his head as he took in the pale face with that cloud of blonde curls surrounding it. Her eyes were closed. Was she even alive? He was frozen into immobility. How could he deal with this when he couldn't even think of the most basic thing he needed to do? When all he wanted to do was crouch down beside Maggie and take her into his arms?

'I've got this.' Tom stepped past him. 'Stay here for a moment, Joe.'

Tom knew who it was. He might not have worked at the Aratika Rescue Base for that long but he'd known Maggie well before that, from taking her patient handovers in the emergency department. He also knew what everyone else knew about Joe's relationship with Maggie and about her pregnancy.

So he knew it wasn't just one patient they had to worry about. It was two.

Maggie...and their baby...

Tom dropped his backpack and crouched beside the paramedic with the stethoscope.

'Accident wasn't high speed from what witnesses have told us,' a young paramedic told him. 'Sounds like she just hit a patch of oil in the road and the wheel slid out from under her. Her name's Maggie Lewis. She's thirty-five years old.'

'I know Maggie,' Tom said. He gripped her shoulder. 'Maggie? Can you hear me?'

Her eyes fluttered open. From where he was, still near her feet, Joe could see how anxious she looked. And how rapidly she was breathing.

'Vital signs?' Tom queried calmly.

'Blood pressure is one hundred over sixty,' the paramedic said. 'Respirations twenty-four. Heart rate is one twenty and her oxygen saturation is...' she looked over at the monitor '...ninety-two percent. That's down from a few minutes ago.'

'T-Tom...' Maggie pulled the oxygen mask away from her face, her voice hoarse. 'Can't...breathe...'

It was the sound of her voice that broke those frozen few seconds for Joe. He was moving now. Close enough for Maggie to see him. Close enough for him to see the very real fear in her eyes.

'J-Joe... I'm...'

'I know.' He put his hand on her cheek for a moment, before replacing the oxygen mask. 'We've got this. You're going to be fine.'

She had to be. That was all there was to it.

'She's got a chest injury on the left side,' the paramedic was saying now. 'Probably broken ribs. She's refused any pain relief because she's pregnant. About seventeen weeks, she said.'

Tom fitted the earpieces of his stethoscope, placing the disc on Maggie's chest. Joe was watching the condensation on the inside of her mask that showed the rate of her breathing efforts increasing. She was also looking more distressed, her head rolling from side to side.

'I think she's got reduced air entry on the left side.' The paramedic was frowning. 'It's hard to tell with all the noise here, though.'

Joe felt like he was having trouble breathing himself. That his own lungs were being squeezed.

'Absent breath sounds, left side,' Tom said quietly. 'And we've got some subcutaneous emphysema happening.' He touched an area of skin where there were bubbles of air marring the smoothness.

'Needle decompression?' The paramedic was turning towards her kit. 'I've got the gear.'

But Tom was looking at Maggie. Reaching to shake her shoulder. 'Maggie? Can you hear me? Open your eyes…'

Joe felt the moment she lost consciousness and knew that Tom had felt it as well. A few seconds later and she stopped breathing. The men exchanged a single glance. The air escaping into Maggie's chest from her lung, probably due to an injury from a fractured rib, had reached a critical level. Her lung had collapsed and the pressure was building. It was pushing her heart towards the other side of her chest and the major veins leading into her heart would be getting blocked. The level of oxygen in her bloodstream would be dropping dramatically. A respiratory arrest would be followed by a cardiac arrest very soon if they didn't move fast.

'Simple thoracostomy,' Tom said, already opening his pack to remove the roll he needed. 'Rather than needle decompression. You agree, Joe?'

Joe could only nod. He still felt as if he couldn't breathe. How could he, if Maggie wasn't breathing? The tension wasn't just in Maggie's chest. It was pressing down on Joe, so hard it felt like something might explode.

Thank goodness Tom, with all his experience and skill, was here to provide a more definitive treatment to this life-threatening situation. He was moving swiftly but calmly. Joe helped position Maggie's arm, lifting and turning it to put her hand under her head. He kept his own hand there as well, covering hers. Just needing to be in contact with her skin. Touching her.

You can't do this, he told her silently. *You are not going to die…*

He watched as Tom cleaned the skin over Maggie's ribs, made a cut with a scalpel and then opened the muscle with some forceps before inserting his gloved finger to make sure he had reached the chest cavity. As he pulled his finger out, he nodded with satisfaction.

Joe felt the movement through his hand and straight into his own chest. He was dragging in a huge breath at the same time as Maggie pulled in one of her own. And then another. The miraculous effect of the pressure being released had her eyelids fluttering again within seconds. Joe had never been happier to see those dark blue eyes so close to his own.

'It's okay,' he told her. 'You're going to be okay. We've got you…'

They had her into the helicopter a short time later.

'I've got her helmet.' Joe climbed in after Tom. 'There's no significant damage and the ground crew said she wasn't knocked out. Her GSC was fifteen on arrival.'

'I think she's been lucky.' Tom nodded.

'We'll be able to check her thoroughly once we've got her into Emergency. Buckle up, Joe. I'll sit by her head. I want to keep a close eye on her in case she starts tensioning again.'

It was too noisy to try and talk to Maggie and Tom was taking excellent care of her so there was nothing for Joe to do but fasten his harness and go along for the ride.

He was still worried about Maggie. Of course he was. Worried about the baby as well, now that the terrifying threat of losing Maggie was receding. It was enough to give him a painful lump in his throat, thinking about how real that threat had been for a minute or two.

Thinking about what it might have been like to lose Maggie.

What was it Tom had said? That you'd know you were in love with someone because it was like the sun had been turned on in your personal universe. He'd just experienced the opposite of that, Joe realised. He'd recognised how dark his personal universe would be if Maggie disappeared from it. How much light and warmth he could lose.

He knew.

He'd known all along, hadn't he? He'd just been afraid to put it into words, let alone admit it aloud. The warmth and light had always been there but he'd thought it was no more than friendship because it was something so different from anything he'd experienced in his romantic liaisons. Now he could see it very clearly for what it actually was.

He loved Maggie.

He was *in love* with Maggie.

He could see her living in that beautiful house with him. As his life partner. His wife. The mother of his child. No…make that children…

Joe still had that lump in his throat as he walked beside Maggie's stretcher as they took her down to the emergency department from the helipad. He stood behind Tom in the elevator and it was then that he remembered something else that Tom had said earlier today—that he would know when he'd fallen in love, but that for a marriage to work it had to happen on both sides.

When the stretcher disappeared ahead of him through the doors of the main resuscitation area, Joe was remembering something else that had been said. Not by Tom. This was an echo of Maggie's voice he could hear in the back of his mind now. When they'd been lying in his bed, having ignored their decision not to let it happen a second time.

Basking in the aftermath of the best sex ever. He could still hear how adamant she'd been in agreeing with him that marriage was not something he had any wish to consider.

'Believe, me,' she'd said to him. *'I'll know who I want to marry—probably within a few minutes of meeting him... It certainly wasn't something I was thinking when I met you, mate...'*

'Joe?'

He could hear Maggie's real voice now. Calling for him.

'I'm here.' He pushed his way through the team that had already been in the resuscitation area, waiting to receive Maggie.

The way she took hold of his hand and squeezed it so tightly gave Joe a weird prickle behind his eyes to go with that lump in his throat that wouldn't go away. It also gave him a flash of something like hope. Hope that perhaps he was important enough for Maggie to want to keep him in her life, even if she would never be in love with him or want to marry him.

'Somebody got that foetal monitor?' The consultant leading the resuscitation team was looking around the room as soon as they'd dealt with the first tasks of reviewing all Maggie's vital signs and then placing a tube to secure the drainage of air from her chest. 'Let's get it on.'

That request changed everything. It didn't matter how Joe felt about Maggie right now. Or how she felt about him. Even the relief that Maggie was breathing well and all her vital signs were within normal ranges got shunted into the background. There was only one important thing to know in this moment.

That their baby had survived this accident.

The realisation of how he felt about Maggie had opened floodgates that had been locked shut for what seemed like his whole life. It wasn't just Maggie that Joe was experiencing such powerful feelings for, was it? It felt like the life of his child was hanging in the balance. His son. Or his daughter. A child that he needed to protect. And that he wanted to be able to love.

'It's on its way from Maternity,' someone said. 'Shouldn't be long.'

'We've got a Doppler here,' Tom reminded them. 'I'll find it.'

Other members of the medical team were still monitoring Maggie's oxygen levels, heart rhythm, blood pressure and other vital signs. They were also doing an even more thorough secondary survey to make sure they hadn't missed any other significant injuries but, as Tom had thought, it seemed that the only real damage had been done when her ribs had been caught by the handlebar of her bike. Tom and Joe would normally have handed over the care of their patient and gone back to the helipad but there was no way Joe could leave and Tom had morphed from being a HEMS doctor back into his usual role of emergency medicine consultant.

He had the Doppler unit in one hand and the small probe in the other. Maggie's clothes had already been cut away and Joe could see that her bump was just starting to show and that made that lump in his throat get so big it was hard to breathe around its edges.

Maggie's grip on his hand, as Tom moved the probe over her belly, was so tight it was hurting but Joe was barely aware of the pain. He was holding Maggie's frightened gaze so he saw the emotion that flooded into her face when the sound of the baby's heartbeat was caught and magnified for all to hear. The rapid, blurred, underwater thump of the sound was well within normal limits. Fast, regular and strong. The most reassuring drumbeat ever.

'You'll need electronic monitoring for a while,' Tom told them. 'At least twenty-four hours, I reckon. But that's a healthy heart rate and you're not bleeding. For now, it looks as if baby's been cushioned well enough to escape harm. Let's concentrate on getting you sorted out, Maggie.'

Joe was still listening to the heartbeat that was the background to Tom's speech. Still struggling to draw in a normal breath. Maggie seemed to be having the same difficulty and her eyes were filling with tears as she broke that eye contact with Joe and turned her head away. She sucked in a breath that was more like a sob, which made her cry out in pain and wrench her hand free of Joe's.

'No X-rays,' the consultant in charge of Maggie was saying. 'But they're ready for her in CT.' He caught Joe's concerned glance. 'We're just doing a scan of her chest, not her abdomen. Don't worry. We're not draining any blood so it looks like a simple pneumothorax but we need to assess the underlying damage and make sure that surgery isn't needed.'

Joe leaned closer to Maggie. 'Want me to come with you?'

She shook her head—a slow side-to-side roll that made a tear trickle down the side of her nose. 'It's okay... I'll be okay. You need to get back to work. I'll text you later, Joe. I'll let you know what's happening.'

Maggie closed her eyes as she was wheeled from the room.

He knew that Maggie would be okay without him because she was surrounded by a great team who were completely focussed on her wellbeing. But he wanted her to need him. As much as he needed her.

Joe had never felt more alone in his life.

CHAPTER TEN

HOW LONELY WAS THIS?

The only light in this private room in the Royal's maternity wing was coming from the screen of the foetal monitor beside Maggie's bed. The steady blipping sound had been turned down so as not to disturb her sleep but she could still hear it clearly and, even in the early hours of the next morning, she was listening just as intently as she had when they'd first checked for her baby's heartbeat in the resuscitation area. The monitor would also record any contractions if the worst happened and the accident triggered premature labour, but Maggie couldn't feel anything happening in her belly other than the weight of the transducers strapped to her skin by the two wide belts.

The loneliness felt like punishment. One that she was convinced that she probably deserved. Telling Joe not to come with her to

that scan— to go back to work, even, as if
nothing major had happened—had been so
hard when all she'd wanted to do was cling
to his hand for every minute of that ordeal.
To have him hold her and repeat the reassur-
ances that all the doctors had given her that
the news was good. She didn't need surgery.
Her baby seemed to be fine. Her chest drain
could come out within a day or two and she
could go home and recuperate with nothing more than sore ribs for a while. She had
been very lucky.

But Maggie wasn't feeling lucky right
now.

She wanted Joe to be here. She wanted to
tell him how sorry she was. For derailing
his life, even though it had been completely
accidental. For not being prudent enough to
have stopped riding her motorbike as soon
as she knew she was pregnant. When he'd
arrived at the accident scene, he'd looked
more shocked than she'd ever seen him look
and that had been almost as frightening as
not being able to breathe properly, as well as
the fear that something terrible could have
happened to the baby.

And she'd seen tears in his eyes when he'd
heard the healthy beat of the baby's heart on
the Doppler. It would have been understand-

able if there'd been an element of relief in the idea that the disruption she'd caused in Joe's life might have vanished but what she had seen in his face in that moment was something she would never have expected.

He'd looked as if their growing baby was the most precious thing in the world.

As if *she* was just as important.

It would have been so easy to believe that look. To trust it. But the rational part of Maggie's brain had ordered her not to. Had spelled out how much harder it would be— when the drama of this event was over—to get back to normal. The normal that she and her baby's father were no more than friends. That they could never be more than friends.

She'd already been struggling, in the wake of that kiss the day she'd gone with him to view the house that he'd bought shortly after that. That had been a physical longing doing its utmost to pull her in and she'd managed to deal with it by staying away from Joe as much as possible since then. To actually believe that he cared so much would not be nearly as easy to escape from. It would be in her head, and her heart, every second of every minute.

That was how she'd found the courage to

tell him not to come with her. That she would be okay.

But she wasn't okay.

Maggie was trying hard not to cry because any sharp intake of breath gave her a stabbing pain in her ribs so she concentrated very hard on keeping her breathing regular and careful. She didn't seem to be able to do anything about the tears rolling slowly down her face, however.

'I'm sorry, Joe,' she whispered aloud into her empty room.

She would tell him again, as soon as they had any time alone together.

It seemed impossible to get any time alone with Maggie over the next week.

Everybody knew that they were no more than just good friends, so it probably didn't occur to anyone that they might want time alone together. In the few days that Maggie was kept under observation in hospital, Joe always had Cooper or Jack or even Andy and Nick going with him to visit her. Or there would be staff members from the Royal dropping in. People like Tom. Or Fizz, who took every opportunity to spend her breaks with Maggie.

'To be honest, it's starting to get harder

to stay on my feet all day.' Fizz was looking very comfortable in the only armchair in Maggie's room, the day after the chest drain had been removed. 'You'll find out in a few months. Thank goodness…' Her smile said that she knew exactly how scary the accident had been for her friend.

Joe wasn't included in that smile. Were people uncomfortable to assume that he was just as invested in this unborn baby's welfare? That it was Maggie that needed the support because she was the one who'd always wanted children?

It was a can of worms that Joe was not about to open. 'How are the ribs?' he asked.

'It only hurts if I laugh,' Maggie told him. 'Don't make me laugh.'

It occurred to Joe that it was a long time since he'd actually heard Maggie laugh properly. Or laughed himself, come to think of it. How sad was that? He shrugged, a smile tilting one side of his mouth.

'When have I ever made you laugh? Serious workmates, that's what we are.'

Fizz snorted. 'Yeah…right…'

Maggie said nothing. She wasn't even smiling as she caught his gaze. Was she remembering what was racing through the back of Joe's mind? There'd always been so much laughter between them. The banter that always provided a chuckle of amusement or two. Jokes that came from nowhere. Tears that came with laughter when they'd discovered just how hot that new variety of chilli sauce was. The way Maggie laughed when she was just excited about life, like the time they'd been bounced around in rough seas on that outing with the coastguard. The laughter that came from pure fun and sheer enjoyment that he'd never, ever expected to be part of a sexual relationship.

Yes...maybe they were thinking about the same thing. Maybe that was why they both turned away from each other at the same moment.

'I get to go home tomorrow,' Maggie said brightly. 'And Don's going to give me a desk job so I can probably go back to work in a week or so. How good is that?'

After she was discharged home, she had her flatmates looking after her and usually had Laura's son, Harrison, cuddled up on the couch with her. The famous taco nights, which had been largely abandoned after Cooper had moved out, got reinstated but Maggie had apparently gone off chilli.

'It's giving me indigestion now,' she admitted. 'I don't think the baby likes it. Oh…' Her eyes widened. 'Just talking about it was enough to make him kick.' She grinned at Fizz. 'I haven't got used to feeling him move yet. It's so weird…'

'Can I feel?' Fizz went to sit beside Maggie on the couch, her hand out to touch Maggie's belly, but Harrison was there first.

'*I* want to feel,' he said. 'And how do you know it's a boy, anyway?'

'We don't,' Maggie admitted. 'Not yet.' She looked up, catching Joe's gaze, and he felt included in that 'we'. There was a softness in her gaze that made him feel more than simply included. As if he was welcome?

He so wanted to be included in the excited quest to feel the baby move but he couldn't ask. Not with the crowd of other people around. That needed to be a private moment. He wanted to be alone with Maggie. To feel his baby moving. To tell her how things had changed in the way he felt about becoming a father now. Maybe even to tell her how things had changed in the way he felt about her because…because he could almost believe, in this moment, that things had changed for her as well.

That something was different.

Something huge…

But how, and when, could he arrange to get that time with Maggie?

'You all packed up yet?' Cooper carried an oven tray with warmed taco shells past Joe. 'It's this weekend that we're all coming to help you shift, isn't it?'

'Yep. I'm good to go. I've hired a van to shift the bigger stuff.'

'I'll be there,' Jack promised.

'I won't be lifting too much,' Fizz said. 'But I'll provide the food.'

'I could help with that,' Maggie offered.

There was a general sound of disagreement. 'It's not as if you haven't already seen the place, Mags,' Fizz reminded her. 'And we know you. You wouldn't be able to stop yourself carting boxes around or something or shoving a couch because it's in the wrong place. You're under doctor's orders to rest, okay?'

'Wait till the housewarming party,' Cooper added. 'You'll be right as rain by then.'

That was it, Joe decided. Once the chaos of the move was over and Maggie had had more time to rest and recuperate, he could invite her to a housewarming party.

A very private one.

* * *

This was strange.

Maggie couldn't see any vehicles she recognised parked in the street outside Joe's house. She checked the text message on her phone again.

Spur-of-the-moment housewarming party tonight. 7p.m. Hope you can make it.

She'd texted back to ask what she could bring.

Just yourself.

He'd added a smiley face to his reply that had made Maggie smile as well. A beat of excitement made her realise how much she was looking forward to seeing him. She'd felt left out of the moving process and that had been days and days ago.

It was a bit after seven p.m. because she'd waited for Laura and Harrison or Jack to get home so that she could get a ride with them but they were late so in the end she'd grabbed a taxi. And now she was standing on the road on a warm, early summer evening and it looked very much as if she might be the first of Joe's friends to arrive for this impromptu party.

Maggie hadn't seen the house since the day of the first viewing and she'd forgotten how gorgeous it was. Magical, almost, with that romantic turret. Late afternoon sun was kissing the faded wooden floor of the veranda and the front door was open a little, as if she was expected. And welcome...

She climbed the steps to the veranda and pushed the heavy door open a little further.

'Joe?'

There was no answer, so Maggie kept walking down the wide hallway of this side of the house that contained the larger of the two apartments. It didn't look like Joe had got very far with his unpacking yet, because there were stacks of boxes in one of the rooms she passed and nothing more than a bed in another room. The big sitting room with its amazing harbour view needed far more furniture than the small couch in the corner and the kitchen benches were covered with crockery and cutlery that needed to be tidied away in a cupboard somewhere.

Maggie shook her head. Why was Joe having a housewarming party when he wasn't anywhere near settled into his new home? And where was he, anyway? The kitchen door was also open so she walked towards that and looked out into the garden. Joe was there, tying a bunch of balloons to the post of a grapevine-covered pergola that shaded the terraced area adjacent to the house. There were tartan picnic rugs on the grassy area beyond the terrace and more balloons tied to the surrounding trees.

Much closer, there was a rustic wooden table that must have been left by the previous owners and Maggie blinked at the plate of food that was taking centre stage. Small triangles of white bread that had been buttered and sprinkled with brightly coloured hundreds and thousands.

Fairy bread?

What sort of strange housewarming party was this? It looked far more like a child's birthday party.

And then it hit her. She remembered telling Joe about her friend Suzie's birthday party, when she'd been explaining why she wanted to have lots of babies. She'd said that there had been balloons tied to trees and fairy bread and chasing games and everything was so much more fun because she'd been part of a big family.

Joe was re-creating that childhood memory but Maggie couldn't understand why.

Or maybe she could, but it was too much to hope for. Too much to trust. Maybe that was what kept her standing there silently, simply absorbing what had been created. For *her*. Feeling her heart expanding with love for this man who'd gone to so much effort on her behalf. And, as if he could feel that love coming towards him, Joe turned and his face lit up with that slow smile that just kept on growing.

'You're here,' he said unnecessarily, walking towards Maggie.

'I am.' Her smile wobbled. 'I heard there was fairy bread.'

Joe was getting closer. Close enough for Maggie to see the way his eyes were crinkled at the corners with his smile and how much warmth was coming from his gaze.

'Am I the first one here?' she asked.

'You're the only one here,' Joe told her. 'I didn't invite anyone else.'

He was right in front of her now. Looking at her like...like he had that day of the house viewing, when they'd both realised they still wanted each other so much, even though they'd agreed that their friendship was not enough of a foundation for anything more. Looking like he had during that rush of pure relief when they'd heard the healthy beat of their baby's heart and she'd felt like she was the most precious thing in the world for Joe. Looking as if the only thing in the world he wanted to do was to kiss her senseless.

'Oh… *Joe*…' This was just overwhelming. There were hopes and dreams and fear and a bubble of sheer joy all trying to mingle deep inside her.

Maggie burst into tears.

'Oh, *no*…' Joe put his arms around her instantly. 'I thought you'd like this. Here…' He led her to the bench seat beside the big wooden table. 'Sit down. Are you all right?'

Maggie tried to nod.

He hadn't let go of her hand yet. 'And the baby? What did the doctor say today? Is everything okay?'

Maggie nodded again. 'She's confident that it's all good.' It was much easier to talk about something clinical than venture onto personal emotional territory that was a complete minefield, so Maggie took a deep breath and wiped the tears from her cheeks. 'Sorry about that…it's just these pesky pregnancy hormones.'

'Doubt it,' Joe said. 'I'm not pregnant and I was worried sick about you *and* the baby after that accident.'

'I'm fine,' Maggie told him. 'But… I'm

still worried about the baby. What if…what if lack of oxygen has caused brain damage or something?'

'You weren't without oxygen for that long.'

'But I was in respiratory arrest. I *stopped* breathing.'

'So did I.' Joe picked up Maggie's other hand as well. 'And I was holding my breath until you started breathing again.'

She could believe that. It was something she'd done when she'd been learning to intubate a patient. Holding her breath once they stopped breathing to be confident that she'd secured an airway in plenty of time to prevent damaging oxygen deprivation.

'It wasn't long enough to do any damage,' Joe added. He was holding her gaze and Maggie could see the golden brown of his hazel eyes darken with some strong emotion. She could feel that emotion in his hands holding hers. A faint thrum of energy that ran up her arms and straight into her chest to squeeze her heart.

'It was just long enough for me to realise that I don't want to live without you,' Joe said softly. 'That I love you.'

Maggie tried to smile but her lips were trembling. 'I know,' she said. 'We're mates. Best mates.'

Joe's eyes darkened even more. 'No. I'm trying to tell you that I *love* you, Maggie. I'm *in* love with you.' He sucked in a breath. 'And I know that you might not want to hear that. And that you can never feel like that about me because you would have known if that was possible a very long time ago but…but I had to tell you. It's been doing my head in.'

The squeezing sensation around Maggie's heart had become a tingle that was going in the opposite direction now. All the way out to the tips of her fingers and her toes.

'I was wrong,' she whispered. 'I love you, too, Joe.'

'Like "in love" kind of love?'

'Exactly like "in love" kind of love.'

For a long, long moment they were silent then. Simply holding each other's gaze. Sinking into the moment of realisation that this was real. That they both felt the same way about each other. Joe leaned towards Maggie but it wasn't to kiss her. He leaned his forehead against hers in a gentle touch that made it feel as if their thoughts were mingling and it felt closer—more intimate—than any purely physical touch.

It was Joe who broke that astonishingly intense silence.

'Are you sure?' he asked very quietly. 'I

mean, you said you'd know if you were ever going to feel like that about someone. That you'd know within the first few minutes of meeting someone.'

'I did say that,' Maggie admitted. 'And I believed it. I thought falling in love was exactly that. Like tripping over something and falling fast. I didn't believe that it could happen slowly. Like a long slide.'

'But...when you knew...that was like falling, wasn't it?' Joe lifted his head. A smile was tugging at one corner of his mouth. 'That's how it felt to me. Like I was falling. Or maybe flying... Terrifying but...the most exciting thing ever, too.'

'I felt like my heart was being torn into little pieces. Because it was only when I thought I'd lost you that I realised what I was really losing. You were so angry with me, I thought I'd lost you for ever.'

'It was the same for me. When you stopped breathing and I couldn't breathe and I could see how dark the world would be for me if you weren't in it any more.'

'I told myself it was just pregnancy hormones and it would wear off,' Maggie said. 'But it's not wearing off and I don't think it ever will. I think it was there all along and I was just too blind to see it.'

Joe's smile was poignant. 'We couldn't see it because we were so convinced we were completely wrong for each other.'

'Maybe it was there right from the start.' Maggie was smiling, too. 'I think I fell in "like" with you that very first day we worked together. When we knocked over that bottle of chilli sauce.'

'And I fell in "lust" with you because talking about making a baby made me see you in a totally different way.'

Maggie laughed. 'And everybody should know that mixing "like" and "lust" is the recipe for falling in love, right? Basic chemistry.'

'So…' The glint in Joe's eyes told Maggie that she was about to get kissed very thoroughly and there was a tenderness in that gaze that made her catch her breath. 'Is this it? The "real thing"?'

'Oh, yes…' Maggie had to blink back tears of sheer joy that sprang into her eyes. 'This is most definitely the "real thing". And I know because…'

'Because you're a *sage-femme*.' Joe's smile had become a grin. 'A wise woman.'

'Don't ever forget that.' Maggie grinned back up at Joe. 'Now, stop talking. Start kissing…'

EPILOGUE

'STOP *TALKING*… Oh, my God… I can't believe I let myself get into this. Never again.
Never *ever* again…'

'You're almost there, babe. One more
push…'

Maggie dragged in the biggest breath she
could as she felt another contraction begin
and then screwed her eyes tightly shut as
she began pushing. She could do this. Joe
had her back.

Literally. He was on the bed with her, sup-
porting her back with his body, holding tight
to both her hands. It felt like they were both
taking part in bringing their baby into the
world. And, a matter of minutes later, there
she was.

Their daughter.

Skin to skin with her mother as Maggie
cradled her against her breasts. Blinking
dark, dark eyes at her father as he reached

out with a single, gentle finger to touch the whorls of dark hair on her head.

'Welcome to the world, sweetheart,' he whispered. 'You have no idea how happy your mummy and daddy are to finally meet you.'

Joe's voice was thick with emotion. Maggie had tears on her cheeks. They were barely aware of the activity of their obstetrician and midwife, who left as soon as they could to give this new little family time together to bond.

'Isn't she perfect?'

'The most perfect baby in the world.'

'Of course she is. Oh…look. She's looking for food already.'

'Takes after her dad.' Joe grinned.

Maggie adjusted the position of the baby and helped her latch onto her breast. 'I think you're right. She's got dark hair. And her eyes look almost black.'

'That can all change. She might end up being as blue-eyed and blonde-haired and as gorgeous as her mum.'

Maggie's smile was misty. 'All parents think their baby is the most perfect in the world but I happen to know that our daughter *is*.'

'And Fizz and Cooper think their little Harley is.'

'He can be the most perfect boy. For now, anyway.'

'Until we have a son, you mean?' Joe's eyebrows shot up. 'Didn't I hear you say "never *ever* again" not so long ago?'

'Did I?' Maggie shook her head. 'I don't remember that.'

'We need more photos.' Joe reached for his phone. 'Oh, I forgot. Fizz and Cooper are hanging out in Emergency and told me to text when we were ready for a quick visit. Are we ready—to let the world in again?'

'We'll have to soon. The grandparents are on their way into town and this little one has an appointment with the paediatrician to get checked. Yes…tell the gang that they're welcome to pop in.'

Laura arrived with Cooper and Fizz, who had three-month-old baby Harley snug against her chest in a sling.

'I can only stay for a second,' Laura said. 'Harry's school called and I need to go and pick him up. He's been sick. *Again*… Oh…' Her face creased as she looked at the sleeping baby in Joe's arms 'She's *adorable* Have you decided on her name?'

'Not yet.'

'We can help,' Fizz offered. 'We're good at names.'

Maggie grinned. 'Says the woman who named her son after my motorbike.'

'I have to run.' Laura leaned over the bed to give Maggie a hug. 'You're looking amazing. Congratulations. Life will never be the same but it will be so much better…'

'This is true.' Fizz nodded. 'You're going to love your maternity leave.'

'I think most of it will be spent finishing our project of knocking the extra walls out in the house.'

'Give me a shout when you need any help.' Laura was on her way to the door.

'Thanks, Laura. I hope Harry's okay.'

'I'm taking him straight to the doctor. I might even bring him in here and get Tom to have a look.'

'Good idea,' Joe agreed. 'I'd trust Tom to check out my kid any day.'

Cooper shook his head as Laura slipped out of the room. 'You can't keep calling her "my kid", you know. She needs a name.'

'You could go all celebrity and name her after a piece of fruit?' Fizz suggested. 'Apricot, maybe? Or Plum?'

'No, no…' Cooper was grinning broadly. 'What about one of those philosophical ones that were on our shortlist? Journey? Or Travel.'

The rumble of laughter in the room was enough to make the baby stir in her father's arms. Joe caught Maggie's gaze.

'Bella's top of my list,' he said quietly.

'She *is* beautiful,' Maggie agreed. 'I think that's the one, Joe.'

'Hang on,' Cooper said. 'We haven't tried other motorbike names yet. What about Suzuki? Or Yamaha?' He put his arm around his wife. 'You know, we might have been a bit selfish to use Harley, don't you think? It was Maggie's bike, after all.'

'Not any more,' Maggie reminded them. 'I've got a nice, much safer little car now.'

'But you loved that bike,' Fizz said. 'Won't you miss it?'

A squeak from Bella prompted Joe to nestle her back into Maggie's arms.

'I think she's hungry again.'

He was being so gentle in moving the baby. Maggie could feel the love in that touch when his hands were between their newborn's soft skin and her own skin. For that moment they were all connected by a physical touch. And more...as Maggie caught and held Joe's gaze for a heartbeat and then another, she could feel how much love he had to give. To her. To their firstborn. To their future.

The question Fizz had asked was still hanging in the air. Would she miss her beloved motorbike?

'I'm not going to miss it,' she told Fizz. 'Not a bit.'

Because safety had just become a whole lot more important to Maggie. She had so much to live for now. So much love to give back.

For Joe.

For Bella.

For her family…

* * * * *